T0161510

CHILDREN
OF WAR

AHMET
YORULMAZ

**TRANSLATED FROM THE TURKISH
BY PAULA DARWISH**

NEEM TREE
PRESS

Originally published in Turkish as *Savaşın Çocukları*, 1997
Published by Neem Tree Press Limited 2019
Neem Tree Press Limited, 1st Floor,
2 Woodberry Grove, London, N12 0DR, UK

info@neemtreepress.com

This book is published with the arrangements of
Telif Hakları ONK Ajans Ltd. Şti

Translation Copyright © Paula Darwish, 2019

A catalogue record for this book is available from the British Library

ISBN 978-1-911107-29-3 (paperback)
ISBN 978-1-911107-30-9 (e-book)

CHILDREN OF WAR

ABOUT THE AUTHOR

Ahmet Yorulmaz was a Turkish journalist, author and translator. He was born in Ayvalık to a family of Cretan Turks deported to mainland Turkey as part of the Greek/Turkish population exchange decreed in the Treaty of Lausanne. He was fluent in modern Greek and translated novels and poems from contemporary Greek literature to Turkish. Most of his original works were written with the aim of making people learn about Ayvalık, the city where he grew up. He dedicated himself to Greek-Turkish friendship and rapprochement.

CONTENTS

This novel, originally written in Turkish, is set on Crete during the period from the late nineteenth century to the years following the First World War. The story is set against a background of real historical events and is based on three notebooks left by a Cretan refugee who died in Ayvalık in Turkey in 1948. The Treaty of Lausanne in 1923 stipulated that population exchanges should take place between Greece and Turkey, leading to the mass deportation of an estimated 1.8 million people. Most had little or no connection with the country they were sent to and many did not speak the language at all.

Maps of Crete and environs

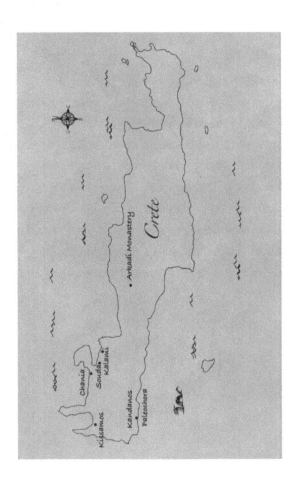

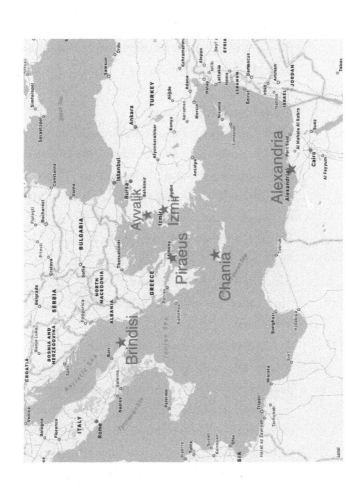

HISTORICAL TIMELINE

69 BC – 1202 AD   At various times, Crete is part of the Roman and Byzantine Empires and also conquered by Arabs from Andalusia.

1202–11   Crete is captured in the Fourth Crusade and sold to the Republic of Genoa.

1212   Crete becomes a colony of the Republic of Venice.

1453   The Ottomans take Istanbul from the Byzantines and begin to expand their empire. It eventually expands to include the lands that make up modern-day Turkey, Greece, Hungary, the Balkans, large parts of Arabia (modern day Iraq, Syria, Palestine and Jordan), Egypt, parts of North Africa and the Arab Peninsula.

1669   The Ottoman Empire takes Crete from the Venetians.

1832   An independent state of Greece is formerly recognised, making the Greeks the first subject peoples of the Ottoman Empire to achieve independence. Its borders did not correspond to those of present-day Greece and the new state sought to expand its borders as they contained less than one third of the Greek population of the region.

1913   Treaty of London – Crete becomes unified with Greece and the Ottomans relinquish their rights to the island. The Greek flag is raised in Chania in Crete.

1914–18   First World War – the Ottoman Empire is defeated. However, the Ottoman victory at Gallipoli in 1915 led to the eventual rise of Kemal Ataturk and the Turkish Republic.

1916   Sykes-Picot Agreement – a secret accord between Britain and France, approved by Russia, to divide up the lands of the Ottoman Empire between them.

1919   The Greek army enters Anatolia, along with other foreign troops, including French, Italian and British. Other parts of the former Ottoman Empire are also occupied. The new Turkish national resistance movement forms in opposition.

1920   The Treaty of Sevres partitions the Ottoman Empire, including parts of Anatolia, between the victors of the war, setting out the boundaries and new countries of the Middle East. It is rejected by the new Turkish national movement.

1920–23   The new Turkish National Army succeeds in expanding the territory allotted to Turkey in the Treaty of Sevres.

1923   The Treaty of Lausanne between the Allies and new national government of Turkey. A new independent state of Turkey is recognised and the new borders of the Middle East are amended accordingly. As part of the treaty, population exchanges of Christians and Muslims take place between Greece and Turkey.

TRANSLATOR'S
HISTORICAL NOTE

Despite the thousands of foreign visitors who visit the Aegean Islands every year, the history of the abandoned villages, mosques and municipal buildings that still bear inscriptions in the Arabic script of Ottoman Turkish is little known outside of Greece and Turkey.

In early history, the island of Crete hosted numerous civil-isations including the Minoans, Mycenaeans and Dorians. It became part of the Roman Empire in 67 BC. In the years that followed, parts of Crete were taken over by Iberian Arabs, but the Romans won them back and the island remained part of the Eastern Roman Empire (Byzantium) until the Fourth Crusades in 1204. The crusaders sold the island to the Republic of Genoa and soon after it fell under Venetian rule, until Ottoman incursions gradually took parts of the island, finally gaining complete control in 1669. The Ottomans ruled Crete until they were forced to leave in 1898, following numerous rebellions against their rule.

Greece, which had also been part of the Ottoman Empire, achieved independence in 1832, although not with its current borders; according to the Encyclopaedia Britannica, it contained under one-third of the entire Greek population of the Middle East. Some Cretans desired union with Greece, which was also trying to expand its territory and supported the Cretan uprisings. The last Cretan revolt sparked an intervention by the 'Great Powers' (Austria-Hungary, the German Empire, France, Italy, Russia and the UK), who sent an international fleet of ships to quell the local insurgency and cut the rebels off from the Greek army. They set up a naval blockade and stationed troops on the island, initially intending to establish an autonomous state of Crete within the Ottoman Empire. All Ottoman troops were expelled from Crete in 1898 and Prince George of Greece and Denmark was installed as High Commissioner with the future prime minister of Greece, Eleftherios Venizelos, serving on his executive committee. This autonomous status came to an end in 1913 when the island was officially unified with Greece. By this time, the island had an ethnically and religiously diverse population, including Muslims and Christians. The First World War began the following year, bringing a final end to the Ottoman Empire, which at its height had included modern-day Turkey, parts of the Middle East which are now Iraq, Syria, Israel, and Egypt; parts of North Africa and large parts of the Arabian Peninsula; modern-day Greece, the Balkans and Hungary, even reaching the gates of Vienna.

With the Ottoman Empire defeated, the Greek army entered Anatolia in 1919, encouraged by promises of territorial gain from the allies, especially Britain. The victors of the First World War divided up the lands of the former empire between themselves and their allies in the 1920 Treaty of Sevres. However, all these events provoked a backlash from a new Turkish nationalist movement, which rejected the treaty and fought to increase the territory allotted to the new Turkey in the treaty. The new movement was victorious, and the borders of the region were once more redrawn by the Treaty of Lausanne in 1923. This treaty also stipulated that population exchanges should take place between Greece and the new Turkey, leading to the mass deportation of an estimated 1.8 million people. As a result of the population exchanges that took place between Greece and Turkey, Anatolia was all but emptied of its Christian "Greek" population, whose presence dated back to 20 BC, while Muslim "Turks" who had lived in the Aegean Islands for hundreds of years were deported to Anatolia. This was the dawn of the nation state in the Middle East and the beginning of the end for the religious and ethnic identities that preceded it, identities that were not defined by national borders.

It is known that following the Ottoman conquest of Crete in 1669, a significant number of the Christian population converted to Islam for financial or other judicious reasons. Intermarriage was also a factor and historians have suggested that up to 40 per cent of the island's population may have been Muslim at one time. Muslims were nearly always referred to as Turks, regardless of whether they had any ancestral connection with Turkey. Historians referring to the reports of European travellers reiterate that the Cretan "Turks" were more often than not Cretans who had converted to Islam rather than of Turkic origin. The character of Mullah Mavruk in the novel also reminds the reader that there were black Cretans, first brought to the island as slaves after the Ottoman conquest.

Anatolia at the time was an equally mixed bag of religions and ethnicities, reflecting the extent and diversity of the Ottoman Empire.

Yet, despite this local mixture, in 1923 millions of people were deported to "national homelands" with which they had, at best, a spurious connection. Many did not speak the language of the country they were sent to and were unwelcome when they arrived. The tragic Middle East wars of the late twentieth and early twenty-first centuries have increased awareness of the Sykes–Picot Treaty, the 1916 agreement that created the nation states of the Middle East by drawing often random lines that cut communities down the middle or closed off areas once freely travelled by Bedouins and other nomadic communities. Even knowing these hard facts, it is easy to overlook the fact that historical peoples did not have the same concept of national identity that later generations were raised with and easy to forget that national identities themselves are constructed from stories that are a function of their time and so anything but timeless. This is where the story of Crete connects with very contemporary issues.

PART ONE

"Don't look down on the first steps
Because from there you will ascend to the palace."

Cretan Folk Poem

1

To be honest, I'm not sure why I was given the nickname "Hassan, the mirror". It might have been because of my immaculately polished boots, smart khaki trousers and walking cane, or perhaps it was the red fez I habitually wore on my head. Maybe it was the cravat carefully fastened under my collar with a long pin inlaid with sparkling stones, or the ring on my little finger set with a shimmering claret jewel that never failed to draw attention? Could it have been the ornate and elegant gold chain watch that always hung from my waistcoat?

No. Somehow, I don't really think it was for any of these reasons, especially when I compare myself to other memorable figures that had been around before me, such as the so called "fragrant Mr Nail", who bathed his customers' feet in special lotions brought from Europe. He used to light up the carnation in his lapel with tiny bulbs connected by a hidden wire to a battery in his pocket. At that time, there were no gas or kerosene lamps lighting the streets, and when the great man passed by the Greek women would lean out of the window to signal to each other that "fragrant Mr Nail" was on his way.

So, in that case, could it have been my neat moustache, swarthy skin and good height that led to the nickname? I just can't work it out. Maybe it was supposed to mean mirror-like but in any case, my real name is Hassan, so forget about the other ones. And don't let the way I dressed fool you into thinking I was one of the wealthy Chanians. I certainly wasn't on a par with jovial Mr Ferid, the entrepreneur, who was one of the richest people in Chania. I was just one of those people who did well by the times and was able to earn a comfortable living, a bit of a night owl who worked hard all day and whiled away the evenings in the tavernas. By the way, Mr Ferid was an incredible man. When the navies of four great countries* anchored in the Chanian port of Souda, and the so-called temporary government was set up, he adopted French citizenship to protect himself and his property. That was during the 1897 uprising, the uprising that started with Venizelos† shouting, "Turks out!" and "Greece is great!"; the uprising that threw us from our homes and villages, forced people into the big cities to try and scratch a living; the uprising that sentenced some of us to die on the battlefield and left others to be strangled in their own fields.

---

* Blockade of Chania 1897: An international fleet made up of ships from Austria-Hungary, France, the German Empire, Italy, the Russian Empire, and the United Kingdom blockaded Crete.
† Eleftherios Venizelos: Leader of the Greek national liberation struggle against the Ottomans and later prime minister of Greece. He was a Cretan and played a significant role in the uprisings.

As well as changing his nationality, Mr Ferid also swapped the fez on his head for a hat. Strangely enough, our women saw the fez as a sign of being a good Muslim whereas the Greeks thought it the sign of a dandy or a womaniser. The first time the great Mr Ferid greeted me, only a mere child at the time, is one of my most vivid memories. He used to pass us on his way back from the farm, ambling along on his Arab horse with a hide as smooth as leather, his booted feet in the stirrups, his hands gripping a silver-handled crop and the hat perched on his head.

"Hello, my boy," he would say in Greek.

In fact, he always greeted me and the family in Greek although we also heard him speaking French. We heard that he was French, and we knew he didn't really speak Greek. Whether he spoke any Turkish I couldn't tell you. I always resented the fact that we didn't really know Turkish, which must have been our original language, our mother tongue. The sultans went and scattered us here like seeds, but they didn't take into account our heritage and future. How much impact could a few Turkish teachers sent over from Istanbul really have? Especially when you think about what kind of teachers they were. There was one in particular, called Master Ismail, who was famous only for his ignorance. Stories about him abounded. One of the most popular ones concerned Master Ismail's friends, who, presuming that his job as a geography teacher meant that he was knowledgeable, consulted him on important matters. One day his friend and fellow teacher Nasip asked him in which direction the Libyan city of Derne lay from Crete. Master Ismail immediately replied, "In the north."

"But dear Master Ismail," replied Nesip, "everyone says that Greece, I mean the place they call Hellenica, is in the north."

Master Ismail was not happy with this response.

"What are you trying to say? Perhaps you think I don't know what I'm talking about?"

"Oh, dear sir. If you say it's in the north, that's where it is, but can you just tell me where exactly is the north?" continued Nesip.

"Let me explain this in a way that you can't fail to understand. On which side is Turkey?" asked Master Ismail.

"To the north, sir."

"And what language is spoken in Derne?" continued Master Ismail.

"Arabic," replied Mr Nesip.

"And Arabic and Turkish are related, are they not?"

"True, sir."

"And which language is spoken in Turkey?"

"Turkish of course!"

Master Ismail's reply was interesting. "In that case, how can you possibly think that Derne is in the south!"

The African city to the south of Crete was apparently to the north just because Turkish and Arabic were spuriously related languages. No doubt the story was a bit exaggerated – and probably made up to deride the stream of incompetent teachers sent from Istanbul, festooned in their robes and turbans – but it goes without saying that the overall situation was far from good.

I'm still preoccupied by this language issue. If I tell you that even the biggest braggarts amongst us only knew about fifty words of Turkish – please don't think I'm making it up. Especially as the number of us who could read and write could be counted on two hands. I'll try to count the ones I knew: there was Tahmişçizâde Mehmed Macit Bey, the leader of the dervish lodge*; Mustafa Tevfik Bey; Ağazâde Mehmed; Fotinzâde Nesimi Bey; Bedribeyzâde Ibrahim Bey; Darmarzâde Ibrahim Bey; Vladimiros, the Greek printer and newsagent who helped me so much when I was growing up; Behcet Bey, who worked at the Joint Emigration Commission preparing documents for those going back to the motherland; Baha Bey, who owned the photographer's in Chania and I also seem to recall another merchant called Celal Bey. They were the people who knew Turkish really well and were able to write. Apart from these and a few others, the rest of us knew about ten to fifteen words and there was a further small number who could maybe muster up to fifty at best. Take Mr Behcet, assistant to the Swiss head of the Joint Emigration Commission, and one of the few who really knew his Turkish: people said he had been educated in Istanbul and Paris. Whereas the rest of us would say, "Get here," he would say, "Come over here." As for the old Greek printer Vladimiros, he had picked up Turkish really well when he was a young man learning his trade in the Tahtakale district of Istanbul. Instead of pronouncing Tahtakale as it's written, he used to enunciate each syllable "Taht-el-Kal-a".

He was one of the reasonable, undogmatic Greeks and I benefited a lot from his great mind as well as his knowledge of Turkish.

---

* There were numerous Sufi orders on Crete, predominantly in the Bektashi tradition.

I almost forgot to add the most important thing was our religion. The one thing that kept Cretan Turks from being paralysed by the fear of falling victim to either individual or mass murder was our religion. Our villages were block-aded, our brothers and sisters were killed, and the priests and schools subjected us to a "Greekification" campaign, but they all came to nothing. Our mother tongue had become Greek, and when we were in mourning, we wore black like the Greeks, but our religion ensured we never forgot our Turkishness. So much so, that if someone asked a Cretan Turk, in Greek of course, "Mehmed, are you a Turk?" the typical reply would come, in very poignant Greek, "I swear in the name of Mary that I am a Turk!"

We were always immersed in both worlds. You can say as often as you like that it is religious unity that makes a nation a nation, as I'm sure in most cases is true, but the Cretans were an exception to the rule and in the most positive way.

We said, "We are Turks!" but that was as far as it went.

It's not that I want to put down our other communities of Turks, I just want to demonstrate how strong both our religious beliefs and our sense of community were. I'll give you an example of how it was that some Cretans didn't think they were completely descended from the Turks.

The first Turkish soldiers that came to the island in 1645 couldn't have brought any women with them; it was some time after the final conquest of Crete, in 1669, when Turkish women came, or were brought from Rumelia and Anatolia; but that doesn't mean to say that all of us had mothers from Anatolia or Rumelia. The Cretan Turks were descended from the Ottoman soldiers that came to the island: traced from a patriarchal line that completely overlooked women. It was through this patriarchy, this discounting of women, that we survived and nurtured Turkish Muslim identity in our children. Sultan Ahmet III's mother, her noble highness Rabia Gulnus Emetullah, was a Cretan. She was from Rethymnon, one of the first places occupied by the Ottoman soldiers. She gave birth to Ahmet in 1673, just four years after the final conquest, so in other words the Sultan's future mother was a trophy of war, born and taken to the palace in Istanbul well before the seizure of Crete, thus making her of Venetian, Byzantine or North African origin. Nevertheless, as I said before, we never forgot our allegiances and that's a fact. During the First World War, the Greeks took Cretan Turks into the army, dressed them in Greek uniforms and sent them to the front. These Turks in Greek uniforms were now Greek soldiers, and as such they were to battle with the enemies of the Greeks, to open fire on them. As it turned out, the soldiers hadn't forgotten their Turkishness. They knew the Greeks' enemies, Germany, Austria and Hungary, were the Ottomans' allies, so they cast aside the rules of war and refused to open fire, saying, "Whoever is on the side of the Turks is with us." They ended up in a military court where they were sentenced to face a firing squad. If I remember rightly, the sentence was never carried out due to pressure exerted by a French general. I'm sure you will remember that it was this war that was the beginning of the end for the Ottoman State.

Let's change the subject. When you think of war, with its dead bodies, destruction, massacres, hunger and sickness – what does it all matter in the end? To hell with it all!

2

Our village of about 300 people was called Kamish and the Greeks called it "Kalami"; both words mean "reed". Years later, during the Second World War, from miles away in Ayvalık in Turkey, I heard on the radio that our village, along with the Kandanos district of which it was part, had been razed to the ground by Nazi war planes because of its relentless resistance to Nazi parachutists.* Just a pile of rubble was left behind. What a bitter twist of fate and history – the place that had spewed our blood for forty days during my childhood was, forty-five years later, being punished by another barbarian force.

It was considered a fairly rich village with its olives, chestnuts, vineyards and vegetable plots. Mostly it produced olive oil and wine but also carob. There was plenty of the fruit we called "*kitro*" or "tree melon" growing there and we used it to

---

* Razing of Kandanos: In 1941, 180 villagers and the homes and livestock of the entire village of Kandanos were decimated by Nazi troops. This was in retaliation against the local resistance movement, which despite being untrained and poorly armed, fought Nazi paratroopers, holding up the German invasion for two days.

make jam. People were always taken aback when they caught sight of it on the trees. Each branch could only hold one of these fruits, which weighed about a kilo, and they needed a little support from the ground to stay attached. Our Turkish girls, the Ayses and Fatmas, gathered olives and worked in the vegetable allotments, while the Greek girls, the Marias, Evredikis and Photinis, harvested grapes for the wineries. The Greeks produced olives and vegetables as well, but they produced much more grapes and wine. Our village soil was fertile. At the edge of the village, there was a small meadow with a huge plane tree in it. Around the area of the tree was the meeting place of two peoples who had grown into each other; I could say peoples of two separate races, but it would be more honest to say two separate religions. There was just one taverna and it belonged to the Greek, Manusakis. In my early childhood, we used to pass by the door on the way back from the allotments and olive groves and I would greet him with a boyish "good evening" which at the time I thought was very grown up. Manusakis would laugh and reply very sincerely, "Good evening, little Hassan."

In later years, as a reward for running to the Greek grocer Hristakis for him, he would place a few pieces of the liver he was frying for the customers on to a coffee-cup saucer and hand it to me saying, "Just taste that, little Hassan!"

Sometimes it was a few whitebait that were brought in once or twice a week by villagers who had been to the seaside town of Paleochora in the south. The journey used to take them three hours but the five or six *oka* of fish didn't lose their freshness. The thought of those crispy fish fried in fresh olive oil! Don't tell anyone I said this, but you don't find whole-some, tasty snacks like that in today's tavernas. The white-bait were held by their tails, two or three at a time, rolled in flour then tossed into a pan of red-hot oil. For lambs' liver the method was different: the liver was placed in the pan in large pieces and once both sides were fried it was split into pieces with two diagonal cuts of the knife then turned over in the oil a couple more times before being served. In the less crowded world of yesterday, the taverna owners were patient enough to prepare mouth-watering, fresh snacks – even in small villages like ours. The two black olives and slice of red radish that he placed carefully on the side of a small plate did more than just make the table look pretty, they also made the wine go down with gusto. At the end of the day, sitting amongst the five or six tables inside, and around the taverna opposite the tall plane tree, you would always find either a Turk playing his *baglama* or a Greek turning the handle of his barrel organ.

Our villagers were respectful and sincere people: there was an instinctive collectivism that meant it was natural for a Turk to help out a Greek at harvest time or for an entire Greek family to gather olives and hoe the land for a Turkish neighbour. The men, with their moustaches worked together in their long boots and the baggy trousers we called "*vrakia*". We were a compatible community where both women and men covered their heads in black if they were Greek and white if they were Turkish. Because of our religious beliefs we were called the Turks, the Muslims or the Mohammedans, but there was no more to it than that. Our holy days were called

Bayram, whilst those of the Greeks were known as *Yortu*, and the mutual respect that bound our communities together was never clearer than at these traditional times. During a Greek festival, the Turks would greet their neighbours in Greek with "Happy *Yortu*," and on Turkish holy days the Greeks would say, "Happy *Bayram*." In the winter evenings, it was usual for the women to visit each other and all of us children loved the visits. I for one was passionate about Aunt Evangeliki's sausage-shaped Turkish delight. When I ate too much, Aunt Evangeliki would catch sight of my mother's reproachful glances and say, "Let him eat, Zeynep – the child loves it," at which my poor mother would bow her head.

I don't know why I'm rambling on about these things; instead of telling you about our house, I'm reminiscing about community relations. Who knows why! Probably because it was an undeniable fact that our communities were utterly melded together; but also because those beautiful years stamped a glorious, indelible impression on my childhood memory. The quarter where we lived wasn't a separate one; we were together with the Greeks. The only separate things were the mosque and the church. I should add that the village imam, Sherif Efendi, and the priest Trasakis always greeted each other pleasantly and asked after each other's wellbeing. At that time, these two holy men had a constructive attitude towards each other, our people got on well, lived in peace and were happy. But later…

Our village house had two floors: to the right of the entrance was a room not much higher than two span from the ground, and in the room after that was the stove and a space to store kitchen utensils. The toilet and stable were in the yard outside. On the top floor were two rooms, one of a fair size and another smaller one. My parents and sister Nazire slept upstairs and I slept downstairs, with my older brother Mahmut, in the small room to the right of the entrance. There was an empty space under our room that provided night-time shelter for the chickens, and first thing in the morning I would stretch my arm through the gap behind the steps into the room, pick up a couple of eggs and take them to my mother who would be working away at the stove. She would add the egg yolk and a generous scoop of sugar to a glass of milk, give it a good stir and then make sure I drank it.

Summertime guests would be seated on the divan by the entrance and winter visitors were sent to the room I shared with Mahmut. The beds were always tidied away in the morning so the place always had an orderly look about it. There were no big changes made at home between winter and summer because the village had a mild climate. In fact, the only significant shift was to bring the small outside stove into the house, along with the kettle that was constantly perched on it, steaming away, stuffed with chamomile, sage and lime leaves for those with a chill, which was pretty much everyone in the case of us kids with our constantly runny noses. At the side of the stove hung bunches of thyme and clusters of garlic and onions. In winter, the house was filled with the scent of healing herbs and bulbs from the allium family, whilst in summer the air inside and outside the house was filled with the sweet fragrance of carnations and basil, planted in earthenware pots and troughs of all shapes and sizes. They were in every sense the typical smells of a country cottage, changing with the seasons.

Now here I am in Ayvalık, a seaside district in Turkey, my motherland, and it fills me with sadness when I look around at the narrow streets and houses with neither garden nor yard; I feel strangely out of place. There are no smells of chamomile, sage and lime in the air – just the stink of mould, which seems to rise up from every corner of the dark buildings, deepening my homesickness. Believe me, I know how pointless it is for me to sit here in the land of my distant ancestors, reminiscing about Crete. So what if about fifteen generations of my family lived there? In the end, the Greeks cried "Turks out!" They wanted to throw us from the land where we were born and bred and that's just what they did. The protestors in Istanbul at the time might have shouted, "Crete is our soul, for our soul we'll give our blood," but as my colleague Vladimiros, the printer, kept repeating at the time, over and over again like a record, "Hassanakis, believe me, Crete is done for! You people don't know what our politicians and church are capable of. They'll stop at nothing. They'll fool everyone and, believe me, they'll throw you all out. One day you'll be saying, that's just what Master Vladimiros said would happen."

So we ended up here, in Anatolia, where the people, our fellow Turks and Muslims, tell us we are "half infidel" or "spawn of infidels". As for our customary diet, full of vegetables and fresh herbs collected from the hills and valleys, they just can't understand it and instead mock us saying,

"They steal from the cow's mouth." They look down on us and keep their distance. Way back in history, our ancestors were scattered far and wide like seeds. We grew and spread, then, just when we were reaching maturity, they ripped our roots from the ground and threw us out. In one sense, it's true that the place we have been brought to is where we started out from all those years ago, but it doesn't compare to the soil, the water and the air that reared us – not at all. Would you call that human fate or the handiwork of those that stand to profit from manipulating two peoples, who peacefully co-exist, into fighting amongst themselves?

My father, Ali Agha, with his huge white moustache and ruddy complexion, wore the short boots characteristic of Crete, a waistcoat and the Greek baggy trousers, *vrakia*, that were just like the trousers we call *shalvar* in Turkish. Doubtless he was a hardworking man, so much so that even after Friday prayers he would go straight to our allotment at the edge of the village and put in a few hours' work. My mother was always telling him he should rest, even if just on Fridays, but his answer was always the same, "It's no sin to work once prayer time is over. In any case, Nazire is grown up now and we're getting her married! And Mahmut and Hassan will need a house, land, animals. If I don't work I don't see that happening!"

He had never been to any school, not even the religious kind, but he was one of those people who was born wise. He spoke slowly, taking care over his words, and earned the trust of his companions with the experience he had gained on the land and from life in general. He used to ask the local imam to calculate how much he should have been paid for the fruit, vegetables and olive oil he had sold; this was how he found out if any of his customers had tricked him. He was an affectionate man. I always remember, when I was about nine or ten years old, it was the only time it had ever snowed in the village, and none of the children even knew what snow was. In the excitement of seeing it for the first time, I spent most of the day running around throwing snowballs, barefoot and bareheaded, so needless to say I caught a chill and ended up in bed. My father had been in the garden, shaking all the snow from the leaves to prevent any damage to the trees as people said it turned the citruses black. In the evening, my back was swollen, and he massaged olive oil into my back and chest saying, "Come on, it will be good for you if I rub this oil in all over," and smiling away he massaged the oil in everywhere, right up to my groin.

He was easy-going, but what stays in my memory about him is that he was the sort of man who made sure he was listened to; that, and his breakfasts. On the days when he wanted to take Mahmut and me to the allotment or olive grove, he would wake us up before daybreak, lay the table with cornbread, or if there was none, some of the homemade rusks my mother made from leftover bread, and some olives taken from the jar. He would fill the large earthenware cups with sage tea and place a few pieces of cheese on the table. After breakfast we set off to work. He never smoked and barely knew the meaning of the word taverna. In the evenings, he drank a huge bowl of milk that we got from Aunt Evangeliki in exchange for some fruit or vegetables as we didn't have any sheep of our own. He was such a strong and powerful man that when he walked, I and Mahmut, who was five years older than me, could only keep up with him by running flat out. In the days before I could read, he told me our great-grandfathers came from Konya in a place called Anatolia. To me, a child who knew nothing of the world, let alone where all the countries were, they were magical words. I have no idea about my mother's roots, no one ever mentioned her ancestors or where they were from. She was a quiet, placid woman who, when speaking to my father, used the respectful term *Efendi*, but more often than not she called him "Agha".

My big brother Mahmut was another matter altogether. He studied with the imam, Sherif Efendi, for two years but only learned to read the Qur'an. He wasn't up to reading much and still couldn't work out the sums for the thirty or forty *oka* of oil my father sold. When he wasn't working on the allotment or olive grove, and had some free time such as on Fridays, he would go and play with his friends on the other side of the meadow. He was tall for his age and had a certain charm about him. By the age of fifteen he was already making headway with the girls. Father didn't let my older sister Nazire help with hoeing the allotment and he would only take her to the land to gather vegetables or olives. She took care of the barn and the chickens at home, or helped mother at the loom, sewing our clothes, sashes, blankets and kilims for the floor. Weaving, weaving, weaving. I don't remember the loom ever being still. Sometimes she even earned money weaving for the neighbours and placed it in a chest to go towards the shortfall in her dowry. She was promised to the Turkish grocer, Arif, and the wedding preparations were underway. She was of medium height with dark features and was a skilful woman, accustomed to housework – the type who would be a great support to her husband. The wedding was supposed to have taken place already but had had to be postponed because of rumours about Arif and a Greek woman. The Muslims had watched the Greeks closely afterwards and started making enquiries about the story. It turned out that Arif's relationship with the woman was little more than tradesman's patter and that there was no shameful scandal behind it. It was concluded that the gossip probably emanated from the Greek grocer Hristakis and it occurs to me now that it was a ploy to prevent Arif going into the village grocery business. Some people were not happy to see him exchange his life on the land for the grocery trade.

To fully explain the twists and turns of our life, I need to repeat and stress some points. We didn't have a school – school for us meant the mosque and Qur'an lessons from Imam Sherif Efendi. But there's more to life than that and it was my father's greatest wish for us to be able to write, do arithmetic, calculate accounts, learn about the world and be generally enlightened children. My brother had read the Qur'an from start to finish, but apart from that he couldn't write a word or do the smallest calculation. When it came to gathering olives or tending to the vegetables, he was in his element and more than capable of amusing himself with the *baglama* he had begged and pleaded for, twanging the strings now and then to release a symphony of sounds. Along with this, he was in constant pursuit of girls and women; that's my strongest memory of him from our childhood.

Mahmut's behaviour had a negative effect on our father, which resulted in him being even more insistent with me. He was continuously telling me that I should study and learn, repeating it as he ruffled his hands through my hair affectionately, or whenever I successfully completed a task for him. He said it with genuine kindness and affection, sometimes using successful local Greeks as an example. He held a particular admiration for those who were able to do bookkeeping. Inspired by what he had seen on his once-in-a-lifetime visit to Chania, he would say, "You need to study, son, because the time will come when those that can't read or write won't even be able to get work as goods porters."

In Chania, he had seen that some of the poor were forced to earn a living from carrying around heavy goods on their backs in the huge reed sacks usually used for food. For now, the porters knew how to get to the houses they were delivering to, but with the population rising, the number of streets and houses was also increasing. One day soon it would be so crowded that the porters would need to be given a piece of paper showing either a sketch or the written address of the customer. To my poor father, who was born and spent his life on the land, this alone was reason enough to learn how to read and write. It was beyond his imagination to consider anything beyond the calculations for the ten or fifty *oka* of olive oil he produced and sold, or the gruelling life of the goods porters.

From the age of ten to thirteen, on days when I was excused from work, I would sling the bag made by my sister over my shoulder, place inside it the Qur'an that usually hung in an embroidered pouch on the wall of the room where my mother slept, and go off for lessons with Imam Sherif Efendi. I read the Qur'an from back to front, learned how to perform the Islamic rituals of ablution and prayer, and how to do calculations full of mistakes, but it was enough to keep my father happy. At least in one way he was satisfied. He took quite an interest as I did my work at night by the light of the oil lamp. In his opinion, I was already a "gentleman", despite my young age.

"Well done, son! Well done!" he would say.

After all the years of his needling away at me, I developed a taste for study. One night as I worked away he said, "You've learned the Qur'an now. I was thinking of sending you to Evangeliki's son, Manolis, to get more lessons so you can learn bookkeeping. What do you think?"

Manolis was consulted the next day and it was decided he would give me maths lessons for half a day a week as well as teaching me a bit about the Greek alphabet. On the first Sunday after this conversation, I went off to Aunt Evangeliki's in the afternoon. Manolis, who was the same age as my brother Mahmut, had studied for eight years. He was waiting for me when I arrived, and we got started straightaway. That day was the first time I saw the numbers we use today. We sat and wrote all of them during that first half-day lesson. I was to work on the numbers and alphabet on my own until the next lesson. By night, in the light of the oil lamp,

I worked away at the homework Manolis gave me on the board my father had bought specifically for that purpose. As I wrote, my hand became more familiar with the shapes, the letters and numbers became clearer, and in the second lesson, surprised at what he saw, Manolis began to take great pleasure in his teaching. He got me to do small additions about chickpeas, apples, beans and olive trees, and as time passed the sums got bigger, growing into a host of subtractions and divisions. He taught me how to do bookkeeping from the smallest to the biggest sums. Using the skills I had learned from Manolis, I went over the old calculations I had done for my father and found my many mistakes. Once, when I pointed out one of my old mistakes, I noticed that my father, who was sitting next to me and seemed to be twisting his huge moustache, was actually wiping away the tears welling up in his eyes. I stared at him as if to say, "What's up?" His eyes glistened and without revealing it to anyone else in the room, he pursed his lips as a sign to keep quiet. As we get older we think about the past. I still don't know if the tears of my elderly father that night were because of the pride he took in my learning or his own sadness at the fact that he had not studied himself.

It was my job to read the Qur'an on Fridays or holy days and to enter the income from our produce and all our outgoings in a large notebook. Although I was five years younger than my brother, the grown-ups of the family took a great interest in me and saw me as his equal. Manolis's family were very touched when I gave him a colourful woollen blanket woven on my sister's loom, because they wouldn't accept any payment for the lessons, saying, "There is no money between neighbours." This gift speeded up my education and I quickly learned to read and write Greek. By the time I was thirteen, I could write a short, albeit basic, piece, and somehow or other, syllable by syllable, read bits of newspapers I came across or paragraphs from Manolis's lesson book. With great patience and tolerance, Manolis pointed out where I had made the wrong emphasis and made me repeat the phrase. Maybe the events I've described up until now aren't that significant to you; but I'll say this – the person who taught me all this was a young man from our town who had completed his education at the Greek school. I could only learn as much as the limit of his knowledge, but the benefit I gained from it went far beyond that.

My father believed we needed to get on well with the Greeks because, as he said, that was what our Sultan wanted. We called the Sultan "Afendimas Padisahis" in our Cretan Greek rather than the Turkish "Padishah Efendi". I didn't know much about it, but there had been something called the "66 riot" and another disturbance three years before I was born. Some armed Greeks had attacked the houses and farms of Turks, burnt them down, committed murder and even burnt people alive. That was how my father explained it to me, but I was a child at the time and I didn't know what politics was. Although, to be honest, my elderly father was no more aware than I was, thinking the violence was due to a few "ill-bred Greeks who had set their sights on other people's property".

It was in the same period that I began to become aware of my brother Mahmut's dalliances with the opposite sex. Naturally, a strapping, swarthy eighteen-year-old village boy couldn't possibly stay single for long. My father was well aware of this fact, but Nazire still hadn't married and that situation would have to be remedied before it was Mahmut's turn. One month, when the pomegranates were in flower, I noticed certain developments regarding Mahmut. I often caught Photini, the widowed wife of Aristides, who had the neighbouring land, gazing at Mahmut. Initially, I was unable to attach any meaning to the looks. We children never referred to Aristides by his name, but always as uncle, until he was sent to his grave by a pain in the stomach. His widowed wife was a voluptuous, attractive woman who was not overly talkative – a woman with no children, who worked away on the land all day hoeing, watering and gathering fruit and vegetables. For some reason, my tanned brother, who had long since developed a fine moustache, was attracting her attention and whenever she got the opportunity she would find a place near the edge of our land to slip through and watch him. Tired and sweating, with her shirt half open, she would observe my brother working on the land from the corner of her eye. Eventually, growing fed up with Mahmut's faint-heartedness, she poured out her feelings in a folk song and I have to say that the Cretans really knew how to make songs:

You are tall, slim and tanned, my love
No longer twelve but some years more
It's time that love came to your door

Mahmut was bursting with excitement. I didn't manage to catch his reply, but she carried on with the words:

We'll swap our hearts, so you take mine
When you do, you'll understand
How much I love my little man…

Afterwards, she took him by the hand, and to all intents and purposes dragged him into the garden hut. About half an hour passed. Then Mahmut appeared, looking around somewhat suspiciously, with one hand fastening the belt around his waist, and the other wiping the sweat dripping from his brow. In the weeks and months that followed, from a hideout in some or other fruit tree, I often observed Photini signalling to my brother, or grabbing his hand whenever the coast was clear, and leading him into the shed. I don't know whether it was instinct, my body maturing or a hereditary urge, but whenever this happened, I felt a pulsing in my loins and pushed my hand down into my trousers in the excitement.

When talking about my brother, other boys of our age simply said, "Mahmut is always chasing girls." But as far as I knew, I was the only person to have seen Mahmut with our neighbour. Apart from that, Mahmut had two sweethearts – Aisha and Ariadne. Both were a few years younger than him: one Turk and one Greek. I had no idea what kind of relationship he had with either of them, but these two names circulated round the mouths of our friends as often as the ubiquitous chewing gum: "Your brother Mahmut was talking to Omer's Aisha by the brook…" "You know your Mahmut? Well, yesterday at sunset he was leaving Ariadne's by the back door."

They would tease me like this, before suddenly pulling the skullcap on my head down over my eyes, starting a frantic skirmish punctuated by our screams as we scampered around in short trousers that finished just below the knee – a poor excuse for *shalvar*. Those were the years! Years when money never cast a shadow over my childhood universe; prosperous years with plenty to eat and drink, full of merrymaking and playfulness.

The first signs that the good days were coming to an end appeared in the face of my father. His brow became more furrowed and he was frequently lost in thought. I couldn't understand why, nor could Nazire or my mother, and as a consequence my sister became concerned about her forthcoming marriage. "Don't worry, my girl," my mother would say, "It'll happen sooner or later! I don't know why he's so distracted all the time. I only wish we knew."

One evening after dinner, without any prompting, my father revealed the reason for his preoccupation. As we were clearing the wooden table in front of the stove, he moved the oil lamp to one side and signalled to Mahmut to stay seated.

"You're the oldest in the family after me," he said, "So make sure you listen to what I'm saying. There's a Greek, called Venizelos, who's stirring up trouble. He wants to get rid of us, throw us out of our homes and country!"

Both my mother, who was clearing the stove, and my sister, busy cleaning the dishes, were shocked, quite apart from my brother who was the next male in line after my father. Where or who could he have got this idea from? This was our father! Our father who had never set foot in a taverna or café, whose life was spun between the boundaries of our house, our land and the olive grove. Our father, who urged us to get on well with the Greeks because it was "what the Sultan wants". How could a man who only interacted with the other villagers to say hello, ask after their wellbeing or chit-chat about vegetables and the weather, who never took without giving something back, express such harsh views? Throw us out of our home and country? Our land, olive groves, our home – didn't these all belong to us? We were all born here, and the land and property had been handed down to our father by our ancestors. Drying her hands quickly on her apron, my mother went and stood in front of my father.

"For the love of God, Ali Agha, what are you on about?" she said. "Is this why you've hardly said a word for weeks? Have you ever heard of such a thing? Where would we go? What would we do for food and water?"

"I'm worried about all that as well," replied my father. "But I've overheard the Greeks talking on the way to the land and olive groves. That's how I know. People who've been greeting and chatting to me for as long as I can remember don't say anything now. Gradually there are fewer and fewer people that even say hello! The rumours aren't pleasant. I can smell gunpowder and blood. Not everyone knows this, but years ago there was a lot of unrest, destruction and killing. In the end, the rebellion* was put down and in time we learned to live with each other again. We might have different religious beliefs, but you know yourselves – we get on pretty well living near each other or even next door."

I couldn't stand it anymore and blurted, "It'll be all right, won't it, Dad?"

"If you look at what's going on, son, it won't be all right. This Venizelos of theirs is provoking people to riot everywhere. This time it's bigger than before. I think these troubles are going to shake the whole of Crete. That's the feeling I get."

As I was asking the question, I thought of Uncle Aristidis's widowed wife and Mahmut's supposed girlfriends, Aisha and Ariadne. All I could think of was what would happen to all of them. Mahmut entered the conversation in a more practical way. "What can we do about it?" he asked.

Nazire had left the dishes and was looking at our father, her eyes misted with tears.

"I came into the world in this house," he said, "in the same room by the entrance that you two sleep in now. This is where I grew up. I got to this age working in the olive groves and on the land. Twenty years ago your mother came into the household as my wife and supported me in every way. She brought you all up. Now there are people who want to spoil it and take everything we have. The reason I'm saying all this is because there's nothing we can do.

---

* The Cretan Revolt of 1866–1869: The third in a series of [Christian] Cretan revolts against Ottoman rule. Locals set up regional revolutionary assemblies and petitioned the Ottoman sultan and foreign consuls in Chania for reforms.

Nothing except protect ourselves and our property if they come under attack."

Becoming agitated, Mahmut asked, "If we get attacked, what are we going to defend ourselves with – sticks and stones?"

Turning to my mother and looking at her with affection, my father said, "Sweetheart, can you get the rifle, revolver and bullets that my father left me from the chest? Mahmut can give you a hand."

When they went upstairs he explained, "These weapons have been in the chest for a long time. Every year, I get them out to clean and oil them then put them back in the chest. I always did it when you were out. I didn't want you to know about things like that. Years ago, after one of the rebellions was put down, our Grand Vizier Ali Pasha said, 'Turks, stow away your weapons,' and so that's what your granddad did. He passed them on to me as an heirloom from our ancestors."

I felt sure Nazire was thinking about my future brother-in-law, Arif the grocer, when she took advantage of a pause in the conversation to ask, "Where's this all going to end?"

"It's turned into a big mess, everything's tangled up in everything else," my father replied. "It looks like we're heading for a lot of trouble. Your late grandfather told me our ancestors took this island from the Venetians, not from the Greeks. Afterwards, a few Greeks came, then more and more, until in the end we were in the minority. This rebel, this Venizelos, is just a young man. He says, 'Turks get out! Death to the Turks!' I'm afraid the attacks and murders have already started."

In the meantime, my mother and brother had come back downstairs carrying two weapons and a pouch of bullets. They placed them on the table. It was the first time I had ever seen a gun. My father asked them to sit down and picked up the small gun he called a revolver. Pointing the barrel towards the ground, he carefully loaded the bullets one by one. Afterwards he took the gun and pushed it down into the huge sash round his waist.

When he started to speak again, his voice seemed to shake. "From now on, whenever we go to the land, we'll carry it in my sash, or maybe to make it less obvious we'll put it in the bag we carry our food and drink in. At night, it'll be under the pillow. We'll keep the rifle behind the entrance door at all times to protect the house with, and we'll hang the bullets on the same nail."

My mother's eyes had glistened with tears as she nervously watched him slip the gun into his sash. "What kind of life is this, Ali Agha?" she said. "How long will this go on?"

"Of course, it's no way to lead our lives. It won't go on for long but, until we find another solution, we have to protect ourselves," replied my father.

"What kind of solution?"

"How can I know that now, my love? If you ask me, the Greeks should catch that troublemaker Venizelos and punish him for coming between us all and making us fight. That's the only way we can go back to our old peaceful life, living side by side. It's not by chance that I hid the guns from you all these years. I wanted to keep the bad things from you. It's not as if we don't get on with the Greeks, is it? Who was it who taught Hassan to read, write and count – wasn't it Evangeliki's boy, Manolis? Is there any better example than that of how well we get on?"

We were all shocked, and silent. My father carried on, "Anyway, we should let Mullah Mavruk and his family know. They need to be aware of what's going on. What I'm trying to say is, there are people who want to throw us out and take our property. If the children of the Venetians had come and done the same, I'd say they were in the right because we threw them out of their homes when we came. But the Greeks came here after we did. They're immigrants like us so it's not right, but we need to get out of here before we get hurt."

My mother repeated her question, "Yes, but where can we go? What's going to happen to us?"

"We'll go north," he said, "From what I can gather from the imam, the Turks are gathering in places like Chania and Kissamos. If we move to the capital, Chania, or somewhere round there, at least we can sail to our homeland Anatolia from there – only if we don't have any other choice, of course. Apparently, there are ships from Crete to Anatolia. If things calm down, we can stay there and maybe even find a school for Hassan."

The words "Anatolia" and "homeland" rushed through my head, blurring one after the other into distant place names I had heard before like "Konya" and "Amasya". With all that I had taken in that evening, I was filled with apprehension, a fear of the unknown combined with the mental struggle of trying to grasp what was going on, let alone come to terms with it. I wondered if the nightmares that had haunted me years ago had somehow been a forewarning, nightmares in which the top level of the house was filled with coffins, some lying flat, some upright. I would wake up scared and sweating. People also called Anatolia "Asia Minor". The simple fact that the mainland was worthy of two different names contributed to the sense of awe it conjured up in my mind.

"Tell us about Anatolia, Dad!"

He didn't speak for a while and looked thoughtful. "I don't know, my boy. I don't know much about it either. Our ancestors came from there a long time ago. I was born here just like you. I've never been there. It's supposed to be a rich country with fertile land, but they say the weather is very cold. That's why people here say, 'If you want to know what cold really is, go to Anatolia!' If we have to leave the island, obviously that's where we'll go. After all, it is the land of our ancestors."

We were all agitated by what we had been told that night; that and the sight of guns. As for me, I didn't want to see all Greeks in the same light and reminded myself about Manolis, who had taught me to read, write and do sums. If they were all the same he wouldn't have done it. He would more likely have made fun of me. Then I thought about our neighbour, Big Hilmi, who lived over the road. Despite being blind from birth and quite an obese man, he always joined us on our trips to the edge of the brook and shared the wild plants and pungent herbs we gathered together. What would happen to him? He did have his own parents, but without us what could he do? How would he get around? What would become of seductive Photini, who met secretly with Mahmut in the hut? How strange that one day, as I had watched her with Mahmut, the feeling of excitement had unexpectedly introduced me to the joy of becoming a man. The Photini effect stayed with me for life; from then on it would always be sensuous women like her that attracted me.

It was the olive grove that my father put up for sale first. The Greeks were reticent for a while. They weren't in the mood for buying and wouldn't meet the price. So much so that my father became increasingly gloomy and pessimistic. The overriding sense that we would be thrown from our home and country was growing, yet we couldn't even save ourselves by selling the olive groves that had been handed down in our family for centuries. To survive in our new place we would need to buy a house and land; it's not as if we could expect the people there to feed us in the name of God or the prophets. In the end, the olive grove went for way under its value and only due to the help of some Greeks who loved and respected our father; or maybe it was all of us they were thinking of. Aunt Evangeliki and her son Manolis spared no effort in helping us out with the sale, especially after they invited us all for dinner one night and heard the reasons for our fears from my father's own lips. Throughout his whole life, my father reaped the rewards of being a good, decent man. He was respected by everyone who knew him. Mahmut overheard a group of Greeks discussing him amongst themselves one day. "How can anyone even think about harming a saint like Ali Agha?" they were saying. "How could anyone try to kick him out? It's unbelievable!"

Even the taverna owner Manusakis came to his aid, although my father had never once been his customer. It was Manusakis who pressurised Kiri Kosti, the owner of the neighbouring olive grove, to make the purchase. Kiri Kosti saw things very differently to my father: "Ali Agha, our Ali, people respect you here. No one's going to hurt you or your family in our village, or on this island come to that. Come on! We're neighbours, don't spoil our special relationship! To this day we haven't caused as much as one olive's worth of bother to each other. In fact, it's the opposite, we've always been a help to each other. Ali, please listen to me, don't throw everything away."

Hearing this emotional plea, my father attempted to hide the tears spilling down his face on to his bushy moustache by wiping them away with his huge palms; but he was resolute in his decision. The olive grove went for next to nothing and soon afterwards, the house and lands came to a similar fate. Kiri Kosti bought the land and Manusakis bought the house for his widowed daughter. They told us time wasn't a problem and that we could stay in the house for as long as it took us to prepare ourselves and start off on our journey.

We bought an extra cart and two mules, but still we could only just fit ourselves and all our things on. My mother and sister sorted through our possessions and gathered together everything we would be able to take; my father and brother bundled them up. According to my father, we had a three-day journey ahead of us. We were to head north to the Kissamos area, which was more densely populated with Turks. We would be nearer to both the capital Chania and, although only by sea, to our motherland, Anatolia. My mother was often completely silent as she gathered together the pieces of our home. At other times she was convulsed with sobs. My father worked on the bundles silently, tying them up then taking an occasional break to pace up and down the house, his eyes misted over with sadness. Then, one evening, in the midst of our preparations, events unravelled in front of us like a piece of weaving snagged on a jagged edge, turning this festering tragedy into a perpetual, bitter scar. We were unaware. There was no way we could have known. Nobody could have known.

Mahmut had gone for a quick stroll around the village that evening, just before the time we always had dinner. The table was prepared but Mahmut still hadn't arrived. For the first time in my lifetime, we had to wait before dinner. One of the most important rules of the house was that we all sat down to dinner together at the appointed time. How could my brother have ignored this rule, especially at a time when our whole world was being turned upside down and our parents were distraught with grief? We sat without eating as the time grew later and later. Unable to bear it, my father went out to look for him in the village. He asked everyone he knew along the way, but no one had seen him. We had waited silently at first, somewhat irritated; but the atmosphere changed to one of fear and apprehension. Nazire and I huddled into a corner. My parents remained on their chairs, sitting silently with their eyes fixed on the ground. I drifted off to sleep.

It was daylight when I was woken up by the sound of repeated knocking on the door. Before I had even lifted my head from Nazire's lap, my father was at the door, pulling at the wooden support behind to open it. A voice was shouting, "Open the door, Ali Agha! It's me, Kosti!"

Our old neighbour, Kiri Kosti, who had bought the land, stood in the doorway, his face ashen. He was suddenly lost for words. My anxious father had a startled look in his eyes, "What is it, Kosti? Have you seen our Mahmut?"

Kiri Kosti was a calm man but now his voice was shaking. "Your boy… your child…"

A picture of that tragic morning is imprinted on my mind; a picture of my father's huge hands clutching the shirt of Kiri Kosti while the screams of my mother and sister filled the air. On the table in front of the huge stove by the entrance, the food lay on plates, untouched as we had left it. The family tradition of eating the evening meal together had been shattered into tiny pieces, taking with it the life of a handsome young man, my brother.

One Friday morning as the sun was rising, we set off on our journey. Along with our Greek neighbours, a group of Turks who were determined to stay on in the village came to see us off. Big Hilmi's mother was there, holding him by the hand. The men hugged my father and my mother cried constantly as she entrusted the keeping of Mahmut's grave to Aunt Evangeliki. "My Evangeliki, I know I've nothing to worry about with you. Please send your Manolis to visit the grave from time to time, even if he can't make it often. Let him carry out my wish in memory of the fact that he was born in my hands."

"I wish you a safe journey!" implored Aunt Evangeliki. "I hope you manage to set up a good home where you're going.

If you ever meet anyone who is coming this way, please tell them to pass on news of how you're getting on."

My mother hugged Aunt Evangeliki again for the last time, before climbing into the front cart next to my father. Still crying, she sang the words of a folk song, bringing tears to the eyes of all those who had come to see us off:

Born on this land where I belong
The hand of fate now moves me on
To end my years on foreign land
A thought that I cannot bear

As the carts began to move, Aunt Evangeliki broke away from the hold of her son Manolis, waving her arms in the air and crying out to console my mother, "Be patient, Zeynep! The time will come when we ordinary folk will come to find each other and be together again!"

As I sit writing this twenty years after leaving Crete, thinking back to the apprehension of a young boy sat in the cart, watching the mules pull us away to unknown, faraway places, the words come alive once more in my mind, and I see Aunt Evangeliki's slender, sun-kissed face full of hope.

"The time will come when we ordinary folk will come to find each other and be together again!"

Neither the profiteering warmongers, the religious men who stupidly supported them, or the politicians could bring us back together. In fact, the opposite became true; we became further apart than ever. Evangeliki, whose age I can only guess by the fact that I called her aunt way back then, must have long since migrated from our earth before seeing the reunion she dreamt of. It won't be long before I follow her, and I can still see no reunion ahead. I don't even think the next few generations will see it. But the important thing is that a Greek woman from a Cretan village, who came from a family where the only person who could read and write was her son, imagined that the day of this reunion would arrive, enough to cry it out in the middle of our tiny community.

I was in the first cart; my mother and father sat at the front and I sat behind, with my back leaning against the bundles and my legs dangling over the edge. In the cart just behind were my sister Nazire and brother-in-law Arif. In a third cart sat our close family friends, the black couple Mullah Mavruk and his wife, Cemile. They had no children and had decided to come with us. They too had picked up on the scent of advancing disaster, had spoken to my father and had made their own preparations to join our convoy. We had stayed in the village for a further two months after Mahmut's body was brought to the house. Manusakis, the taverna owner who had bought the house, told my father we could remain in the house for as long as the period of mourning lasted. While Imam Sherif Efendi was preparing Mahmut's corpse, he noticed a suspicious purple mark and a fine line of blood on his left breast. At a closer glance, he saw that a long spike had been thrust into his chest. To put it plainly, my brother was killed by a long spike pushed into his body as far as his heart. But who would do such a thing? Why, and how? That bit we couldn't figure out. I was a child and I had lost a brother I loved and admired, but for my parents it was worse; for them it was a double blow. Not only were they being torn from their roots, but they had also lost their eldest son, and in such a way that they would never be able to forget.

Forty days after the terrible event, my parents accepted Arif as a groom and as a son, partly for the sake of Nazire and partly because of the extra physical strength he would add to the family. He had no one else anyway. The village imam performed the wedding ceremony and Arif moved in with us until it was time to go. The marriage would never have taken place so quickly if it hadn't been for the need to flee and the raw, bitter wound left by Mahmut's murder being inflicted on us in quick succession. No doubt Nazire would have been happier if the faces of my parents had not been stoically withdrawn and on the verge of tears at the wedding. But even despite the sadness that overshadowed the occasion, my sister acquired a distinct fresh glow that wasn't there before. Her life would soon be completely overtaken by the struggle to survive.

3

Our convoy of three carts had only been on the road about half an hour when five Greeks, armed and on horseback, cut in front of us.

"Ali Agha!" one of them shouted, pointing his gun towards the sky.

"What's this, an imperial procession? There's something you need to know. Your people aren't at Kissamos,* they're gathering not far from here, in Kandanos.† Kissamos is a long way and Kandanos is nearby. If you want to get to your people in one piece, turn your cart towards Kandanos."

They disappeared as quickly as they had come. We were all shocked. They not only knew my father's name but also where we were going. My father shared his thoughts with us all: "All the signs point towards a huge storm. Those horse riders didn't kill us, but they could have. Kandanos is about an hour away instead of a three-day journey – let's go and see what's going on. May God help us!"

---

* Location of an Ottoman garrison.
† Location of an Ottoman garrison.

So we changed direction and travelled for another hour, reaching Kandanos before midday. It wouldn't be long before we would find ourselves wishing we had stayed to be slaughtered in our own village. Kandanos left us fatherless and destitute.

At the border of Kandanos, it was Turkish guns that stopped us... Who were we? Where had we come from? They needed weapons for defence, did we have any? My father showed them the rifle he had stuck between two bundles and the revolver in his belt. They rode in front of us, showing us the way, then got us to close off one of the roads into the town with our carts – we weren't to allow anyone in but Turks. Mullah Mavruk had brought along a gun left to him by his father, but he was afraid of guns and had never used one, so it was given to Arif. Neither Mullah Mavruk's family nor mine could understand or accept the barbarity of having to kill to live or live to kill. It was not something we associated with the human race. We were all against killing and death.

As soon as we entered the town, we realised there were only Turks living there. Along with others like us who had fled from the surrounding villages we were altogether around 750 to 800 people. The new arrivals were huddled in groups of makeshift shelters around the village, together with their animals and whatever belongings they had been able to bring with them. There had been twenty-five Greek families living alongside the Turks, but hearing news of the uprising, they had moved to areas where there were more Greeks. They had uprooted their entire households just to move a few miles within the same border. That just about summed up the desperate situation; first it was Venizelos shrieking

"Turks out!" at us, then it was his armed supporters, ready to kill us without batting an eyelid. The ground was being prepared for an attack. Although I don't know why I'm saying "prepared"… Considering that our worldly possessions had been sold for next to nothing, and sometimes literally for nothing, and that we were as good as driven from our homes: that was clear proof that their plan to get rid of us was already in motion.

As we rushed to lay down blankets and mats to set up camp next to our carts and find a place for our mules under the nearby trees, we were approached by a short man, who introduced himself as Hassan, commonly known as "Daggerlad". He told us that he had been given the nickname due to his preference for using the all-purpose Cretan dagger over a gun, then went on to tell us about Kandanos and the Turks that had gathered there.

"I'm a local," he said. "There are about 800 people here, including those like you who've fled from the surrounding villages. Now let me tell you something else – a Greek officer called Vassos has sent 17,000 soldiers from Greece to join up with the armed rebels on Crete. Some of them are on their way here now."

"Don't say that, for God's sake!" said my father, incredulous, "Daggerlad, are you making this up? What are we going to do?"

With a manner noticeably sterner and more hardbitten than my father, Daggerlad replied knowingly, "There's nothing we can do now, Agha. Keep on as you are, and make sure you don't go anywhere without a gun!"

"I'm sure the Padishah Efendi in Constantinople* will come to our rescue," my father insisted.

"Agha, I think he's a bit busy at the moment; there's not a whisper from that quarter."

We were all taken aback by this reply. The Padishah was the greatest power – he wouldn't leave our people like this. Yet here was this slip of a man with two daggers stuck in his belt saying all manner of things about the Padishah Efendi! We were astounded.

Daggerlad was a shrewd character and evidently read our thoughts from the expressions on our faces: "Not long ago, I thought of heading to Chania. I stayed only two days, and that was hard enough. There's no relief for people there either. Apparently, the reason the Greeks are getting excited is that the Padishah Efendi's navy is weak. That's what they say. How should I know? When the time comes, I'll get these things out of my belt. This dagger is my sweetheart. I only use it in hand-to-hand fighting. Here's a small slim dagger as well. Before the shooters can even point their rifles, I've already jumped in and finished the job! Well. Enough talking. I've told you as much as I know. From now on, we've got our work cut out! All right, now look after yourselves."

Daggerlad went off, leaving behind him a mass of anxieties.

After the ordered and busy life we were used to, living in a tent was soul-destroying. The bitter loss of my brother rubbed salt into the wound. Our animals were left unattended by the trees as we huddled in frightened anticipation

---

* The Sultan of the Ottoman Empire (Istanbul).

inside the small tent, forced to rush off to the ditch to meet our basic needs. It was unbearable.

Daggerlad's words came to fruition one night, five miserable days later, when an armed Greek force in their thousands completely surrounded Kandanos. They even had cannons. How quickly the news spread. The gun barrels of the Turks protruded from house windows, doorways, rooftops, street corners, the edges of chimneys and from the carts guarding the roads. But not a trigger was pulled – neither by the Greeks nor us.

During the night, not one gaslight or oil lamp was lit; a dense blackness fell on the town. The silence was so intense, it seemed to shatter our eardrums. Terrified of weapons, our family and friends were completely drained by this nervous anticipation. Mullah Mavruk and his wife, dressed in black, were barely distinguishable from the thick blackness of the night. My father pointed his rifle out into the darkness from between the wheels of our cart – a giant of a man with eyes full of tears. My brother-in-law, Arif, held his gun more resolutely and with more care. My sister, Nazire, stayed at his side.

The fear and apprehension of night passed into morning without the firing of a single weapon. The heat of the rising sun dissipated the deathly silence and a hum began to sound from one end of the town to another. People were sharing their fears and unravelling the consternation of the tense night. But the hum of chatting was interrupted by the ear-splitting metallic explosion of a howitzer shell. Two people were killed instantly on the spot, the leg of one of them blown apart from the knee down. The panic caused by the proximity of death turned into insurrection. Our people had already endured random attacks, mass murders and expulsions; to come face to face with death in the place they had sought refuge drove them into a frenzy. Some entreated God to deal with the perpetrators, while others like my father, muttered, "Our great Padishah's soldiers will come and punish them," dreaming that at any moment, the Ottoman soldiers would appear dressed in red fezzes with bayonets strapped to their rifles. Others trusted in their own fists and guns, bawling, "We'll show you, you Greek scum!"

The enemy was delivering us a message. The only problem was interpreting what the message was. It might have meant, "You can't run away now, we're going to kill you all," or "As you can see, we've surrounded you on all sides. Eventually you'll run out of food and water and die!"

The bellows of those baying for blood mingled in with the cries and screams of the relatives of the victims. As for me, still only part way down the road to becoming a man, I left the family and wandered through the crowds to see what was happening. Suddenly, I bumped into Daggerlad.

"My little namesake," he said, "you shouldn't be hanging around this sad place, you'd be better to stay at your dad's side. This isn't a sight for your eyes."

"After my big brother was killed, something happened to me, Uncle. I know I'm sad, but I don't feel much right now."

Daggerlad looked disturbed by my reply. "Look, my boy," he said, "don't become hardened so quickly. When you've done and seen more, when you're older, then maybe it won't seem out of place. But not now."

I was forced to go back to my family without watching the burial of the dead. I was worried that Daggerlad might become even sterner with me or tell my parents what I'd said. I didn't want my father to be any more upset or to risk losing his respect.

The Greek blockade was in place a considerable distance from the village. Peering into the distance, you could just make out the brigands on the horizon. Emboldened by the space between us and them, my mother took me and Nazire with her to pick leaves and herbs in the fields around the village. Our insides were parched from eating nothing but dried fruit and nuts for the past two days. At breakneck speed, we filled a huge bag with a mixture of winter plants, expecting to hear more gunfire at any moment.

At dusk, we once more heard the metallic roar, just as we had in the morning. This time it was the courtyard of the mosque that exploded. As everyone had taken cover at home, or bedded down somewhere to point weapons at the enemy, this time there was no injury or calamity. Afterwards, from our shelter we saw a group of people knocking on doors and passing on some news. They muttered to the men pointing rifle barrels out from behind the corners of buildings, to the children keeping guard in the ditches and to the families holding the roads with their carts. The bustle of communication spread from one end of the village to another, eventually reaching us: someone called Daggerlad was going to seek revenge for those who had been killed in the morning. Taking just one person with him, he would make his way behind enemy lines and knife the enemy. We were told to be ready for the enemy's swift retaliation.

After two shells, two deaths, one seriously injured victim and the news that Daggerlad would try to breach the Greek lines, a terrible sense of foreboding mingled into the chill winter air of the second night of the blockade. We struggled to stop our bodies from shivering. Now and again, someone dashed to the bushes to empty their stomach from one end of the body or the other. Not that they could go far; the Greeks would see to any solitary Turks they caught by severing their heads. The men committing these chilling murders were the brigand leaders, referred to as "captains". I can still recall the names of the bloodthirsty thugs who were talked about during the blockade: Captain Frangiskoz and Captain Kamaryanos. As if butchering people was an honourable deed! After the tranquillity and good relations of our village, no one in my family could comprehend the savagery that had suddenly surrounded us.

"We were all getting on fine together only yesterday; where did all this violence come from?" said Mullah Mavruk. He and his wife Cemile, who was like an aunt to us, thought exactly the same. Was it something to do with both of them being black? Who knows? What we did know was their affectionate nature, their fear of guns and that they were the gentlest type of people, who couldn't even bear to crush an ant.

Here we were, about 800 people facing the massed guns of an unknown number of Greek brigands. The tension rose to a climax after midnight, when gunshots sounded far off in the distance, then a metallic boom that shattered the night, followed by the crash of tumbling walls from the nearby mosque! It all happened in a flash. Then another shell! The crash of walls, the explosion and heart-wrenching screams all seemed to merge into one. People were running to the rescue. This time, one person had been blown apart and there were three injured from one house. Towards morning, Daggerlad came to our tent. Our faces were ghostly white from fear of the shells and the strain of clutching weapons for hours on end with no sleep.

"I'm tired," said Daggerlad, "and hungry."

"Aren't you going to tell us what's going on?" replied my father. "We're desperate to know. We heard you were going to the enemy lines. Did you do it? What happened?"

My mother placed a bowl of food and a piece of bread starting to go stale in front of Daggerlad. She had mustered the broth up from the various plants we had gathered. The small man, sitting cross-legged on the bare earth, tucked into it ravenously. Afterwards, wiping his mouth with the back of his hand, he said, "Agha, don't let me say too much in front of your child and the women. We visited the Greeks. I took one man so he could be my witness when I returned. We made good use of the knives we were given, even in the dark of night. I said 'we', but really, I mean 'me'. The man I took with me almost died of the jitters on the way. That's all I'm going to say. I think it's enough. Five knives right on target. Five less enemies. On our way back, when we got on to the flat, they saw us and opened fire. They sent a couple of shells, but they were wasting their time. We called it a day after that."

My father spoke in earnest. "Look, Daggerlad," he began, "none of this is good. They came to us, they killed our people with shells. You went to them to get revenge, to get even. Then, you killed. Next time, they fired more shells and killed more of us. Lots of people are badly hurt. But remember how it was before? We respected each other, we got along fine. Now they're kicking us out and killing us along the way. And in return we kill them back. Where's all this going to end? Have you ever thought about that?"

"Maybe we're paying the price for sins that others have committed?" Arif said.

"That's what I'm thinking, son," replied my father. "Me – who's never been to school and knows nothing but growing olives and vegetables. Me – Ali Agha, what can I say? We're ordinary people. I don't know anything, but the way we're being treated now makes me ask the same question: what kind of sin is it that we're paying for?"

Mullah Mavruk joined in: "Maybe it was the Turks who sinned when they went off to the place called Europe, where all the people are non-believers. Who knows? I mean, it happens doesn't it? They did something bad and now we're being punished."

"I'm not accepting any excuses," Daggerlad retorted. "I don't really know what you're talking about. In this world, what goes around comes around. I can say that much because I know it's true. We'll give as good as we get!"

My father insisted in the face of this stubbornness, "Daggerlad, Efendi, everything you're saying makes sense. What we're saying is that, no matter who started it, it needs to be stopped. Let's draw a line under the past and live in peace. Whatever pain and tragedy there is in the past, both sides should forget it for the sake of peace. That's what we're trying to say."

Daggerlad was unswayed: "You keep thinking that if you like. The Russians, British, French and Italians have had enough of Greece and the island Greeks doing what they want and they are fed up with our Padishah Efendi being asleep. That's why they've sent warships to Chania. The island Greeks started a rebellion in Chania that's spread across the whole island with the help of Greece. This blockade is the upshot of all that. Supposedly, the battleships of the four great powers are going to stop the Greeks. Words! The only thing that can stop the rebellion is us, fighting back."

4

Hours turned to days, days to months, filled with the hiss of bullets that sometimes found their victim, or sometimes passed by and exploded as if the brigands were saying, "Watch out, we're here!", and filled with corpses hit by unpredictable shellfire that sometimes rained day after day, only to stop for a day and start again…

The blockade stayed in place. The food we had prepared for the journey was long since finished. There was no way in or out of the town. No one could get out to their fields or vegetable plots. To try leaving the town required fearless bravado. At the beginning of the blockade we were able to find food from the shops or various other sources, but as the blockade stretched into a month, food became scarce. We finally understood the message: they would starve us to death. Any who were brave enough to try and escape would be finished off on the road out or before they even got that far.

The dried foods the townspeople customarily stored away over the summer and that were meant to last the winter had also run out. The edible winter plants growing in any wasteland out of the view of the blockaders were also just about exhausted. In the dark of night, some reckless madcaps tried to bring back vegetables from the closest plots, wriggling along the ground to avoid the eyes of the enemy. Instead of three meals a day, we had only one plate of herbs or vegetables stewed in olive oil and instead of a fresh loaf, a hunk of hard, dried bread. We lived on this – alongside the dead and the wounded – for forty days. The forty-third day of the blockade fell on a Friday. The Friday that took my father.

Our people, the Turks, had been heartened by the fact that although the shellfire had reached the mosque courtyard, the interior remained undamaged. Assuming this to be the absolute limit of the shells' reach and believing the roof could not be hit, my father and Mullah Mavruk went off to Friday prayers. Then, right at prayer time, came the sound of three shells one after the other... followed by shouting, screams and frenzied villagers running to and fro. Arif and I ran towards the mosque. People were bringing out the dead and wounded. There was no point in cursing the enemy now. Ten people had been killed and one was my father. There were seven wounded, all of them old men.

I was a teenager and I had lost the father who had showered me with unconditional love and supported me in everything I strived towards. Stunned by the momentous loss, too great to put into words, my mother and Nazire pulled their *yashmaks* across their mouths, their bodies convulsed with sobs, and took my father off to his grave. The mounting number of deaths had by now exhausted the town's supply of the cloth used to make death shrouds. From in amongst the pile of possessions on our carts, my mother managed to extract her husband's long nightshirt so it could be used to wrap him in. The civil war had even denied my peace-loving father a death shroud. Neither could a coffin be found. His body was laid on a four-handle wooden stretcher and covered with a rug in place of a proper shroud.

The forty-sixth day of the siege fell on a Monday. As the sun rose in the early hours, the sound of trumpets and horns broke the usual silence of the morning's armed standoff. The sudden clamour of panicked voices rose to a crescendo:

"What's that? What's going on?"

"Wake up! The enemies have got into the town!"

"Get up! They're going to riddle us with bullets!'

Daggerlad, who had taken us under his wing since my father's death, suddenly appeared at the side of our carts. "Don't be afraid," he said. "That's the Italian and French soldiers coming to rescue us from the Greeks."

"Maybe so," responded Arif, "But they're non-believers too! What are they doing here?"

"They're from the armies of the four great powers," said Daggerlad. "Their ships are anchored at the Port of Souda in Chania.* They'd hardly arrived when the news reached here. I told Ali Agha, God rest his soul. Come on, there's no need to panic now."

The "pasta-munching" Italians and "wine-swilling" French,

---

* In March,1897, Russian, Italian, British, French and Austro-Hungarian troops completed the evacuation of over 1,500 Cretan Muslims and several hundred Ottoman soldiers from the village of Kandanos in south-west Crete, then under siege by Christian Cretans supported by Greek manned artillery.

as Daggerlad described them, came with bayonets on their rifles, formed a pocket to protect us against attack and in a convoy took away the remaining 700 or so Turks, some on foot, some together with their horses, donkeys and carts. On the way we learned that there was trouble in Chania, so they were taking us to Kastelli, on the Bay of Kissamos, to the west of Chania. We were to stay there for a while until the situation calmed down. Our journey lasted two days and two nights. On the way, two of the old folk died of exhaustion and were buried in graves made at the side of the road. This delayed the convoy by a couple of hours. We were suffering from horrific hunger and tiredness. The deaths in Kandanos, the fear and hunger and, to crown it all, the physical fatigue of the journey, had separated these two poor wretches from their souls in an alien place, rather than in their own beds. The feelings of hate and revenge were sharpened by the exhaustion of being hounded from home and surrounded by death. But I was my father's son, and his conciliatory nature was part of me too; I couldn't find a place in my heart for the way the others felt, for their hate and revenge. This pointless fight had to be brought to an end; this was no remedy. But could a teenager like me have said anything? And if I had opened my mouth, could I have got them to listen? Even if I had caught their attention for one minute, wouldn't it have been seen as speaking against the interests of this community of Turks? The Greeks didn't know when to stop; they were expelling and killing without mercy.

At Kissamos, if you had money it was possible to find food. The district of Kastelli on the fertile gulf was a prosperous place with plenty of fish. Filling our stomachs with plates of boiled chicory, wild radish, cauliflower and mustard greens accompanied by a few pieces of fried sea bream, sardines or whiting gave us enough comfort to see the days ahead with more hope. Would the expulsions, murders and exhaustion come to an end in Chania? We hoped so, but we had no real idea.

A week later, after walking from dawn until dusk once again under the protection of the French and Italian soldiers, we arrived in the suburbs of Chania, in a place they called Varusi. They said we could stay and settle if we found a job and house in the city. The French and Italian soldiers who had accompanied us returned to their ships of wine and pasta, and my twenty-six-year life in Chania began. I stayed from 1897 to 1923. It was here they gave me the nickname Aynakis, meaning "little mirror", a mixture of the Turkish word for mirror and the Greek ending meaning "little", and it was here I learned the rough and tumble of adult life.

5

My mother used to select the best large dried figs and fill them with walnuts. The figs, which we called *sikula*, were packed on to a clean tray which was then thrust into my hands. I would lift the tray up to shoulder height, steady it there with both hands and set off along the road from Varusi to the city centre. Shops, coffeehouse, tavernas – I visited every one of them until the tray of figs was empty and I could drag my weary feet back to the small summerhouse that was now our home. No sooner had I handed over my earnings than my mother would send me back to the grocer again to buy more walnuts and the fattest figs I could find, so she could begin to prepare the next day's wares. The few coins remaining after the walnuts and figs had been bought went towards our household expenses. When the fig season was over, my mother made sesame halva. When that was finished, there would be pumpkin seeds, early plums, early green almonds or other seasonal varieties of the snacks we called "*pasatempos*". I sold most of the snacks made from these freshly harvested fruit and nuts in the tavernas of Chania.

The money we got from the trays of snacks that I balanced on my shoulders or head were essential for the survival of our household and my work required the utmost diligence and discipline. This didn't go unnoticed in the area. Among my regular customers were the workers at Yusuf Kenan Printing House, Baha Bey, the photographic studio owner, and the Greek printer, Vladimiros. Sometimes it was just one and sometimes more, but every day without fail they bought whatever I was selling. They knew that we had been forced to leave our village in the south, that we had been under blockade for forty-five days and that my father had been killed in the shelling. I sensed that they had great sympathy for us.

The typesetters at Yusuf Kenan showed me some huge letters of the alphabet. After I told them what they were, they asked me to read some text. But I couldn't manage it. I had learned how to read the Qur'an, because that was just a matter of memorising the meaning. When it came to anything else, it was impossible. The other thing I knew was how to count. I watched Baha Bey as he photographed the Greeks, with hats poised on their heads, or the Turks dressed in a turban or fez. With a mixture of wonder and embarrassment, I saw the pictures on the walls of the studio showing voluptuous women with their laced ankle boots and legs naked to the knee, their breasts half-revealed and heads uncovered. It was a world that we Cretan villagers had never seen and were totally unaware of.

Some days, when I sold my goods early, I would go and watch the intricate work of the typesetters, often taking the composing stick and passing the rest of the day trying to assemble a written text out of the huge letters that were put in front of me. For a long time, I continued with this exercise, which increased my knowledge and experience. At the start, I was all over the place and made a myriad of mistakes. I grew weary from the effort of trying to match each letter in the writing with one of the letters from the typecase, and my fingers turned black from the printing ink. It all earned me a scolding from my poor mother, not only because I was late home, but also because it was important for food-sellers to have clean hands. After attempting to clean them with kerosene at the print house, the process continued at home with endless rounds of soap being deployed in an effort to blanch my blackened fingers.

My interest in printing continued for some considerable time, after which I made myself useful at Baha Bey's photographic studio, sweeping the floor, emptying out buckets of chemicals from the darkroom and watching out for customers at the door whenever Baha Bey had to go out. I also learned to use a mirror to refract light from the outside door on to the individuals or couples coming to be photographed, observed how the special glass used in filming was bathed in the dark room and how the photos themselves were printed.

The orchard summerhouse that was now our home had two quarters and I stayed with my mother in one side while my sister and brother-in-law lived in the other. One year after our arrival, Nazire gave birth to her first child, who she named Mustafa. Arif worked as a farmer for three years and for extra money hired himself out to plough fields with the mules that had drawn our carts to Chania. In his free time, he went into the city in search of a shop. He was a grocer by profession and that's what he hoped to carry on doing.

Mullah Mavruk and Aunt Cemile hadn't been able to find a place to live immediately. After camping out in their cart for months after we arrived in Varusi, they eventually moved into a tiny house, just five hundred metres from ours. They had set off from the village with us, pretty much on the spur of the moment, and hadn't been able to sell any of their possessions. In our home village, working on their own land had afforded them a comfortable life, but now the husband and wife worked as casual farm hands for others in and around Varusi.

As for Daggerlad, two or three years after we settled in Varusi, I bumped into him in a coffeehouse in the Splantzia district of Chania. I gave him one of the sesame halva from my tray, and he ordered me a *sumada* syrup made from almonds and sprinkled with cinnamon. "Look at us, my boy," he began. "The Greeks chased us from our homes and fields, and it looks like they've calmed down for now, but because of all that here you are selling sesame halva. How's it going? Are you at least managing to get by?"

"It's not bad, I suppose, but we were much better off on our land in our own village," I replied.

As he was leaving, Daggerlad again offered his support: "If you ever have any problems, leave a message for me at one of the coffeehouses here. Helping out good people whenever it's needed is something that makes me a happy man."

The life of a travelling seller had become my school: and what things I learned at that school, what things... It seemed the violence that had gripped the island, even as far as our little village, stripping us of our home, had first broken out here in the capital city. Yet it was in this very city, the cradle from which the barbarity had first sprung, that I was trying to lay down roots. In the meantime, I witnessed our Ottoman soldiers leaving the island. At the first New Year celebrations immediately after their departure, I heard the Greek brass band playing a Greek march with the words, "Kill the Turks, slay the tyrants!" It was so loud, it seemed they were trying to burst our eardrums. Then came the appointment of Prince George of Greece* as High Commissioner of the island under the oversight of Russia, Britain, France and Italy, following which I painfully watched Constantine,† who arrived on a warship, raising the Greek flag over the island. I saw the elections for the National Assembly of Crete,‡ whose objective was to make Crete part of Greece, and the efforts of the few elected Turks to defend the rights of the island Turks and the Ottoman state.

They were hoping to melt us into their own national identity and destroy us by replacing the word Turk with Muslim. In short, they wanted to convert any of us that they hadn't manage to chase away or kill into Christians. One day, while I was in Splantzia Square buying cheese at the shop of Shaban Agha, a grocer and dairy farmer, his neighbour, the cheese wholesaler Nikola Kokoloyannis,

---

* Prince George of Greece and Denmark, Son of George I of Greece and Olga Konstantinovna of Russia, served as high commissioner of the Cretan State during its transition towards independence.
† Constantine was the commander-in-chief in the Greco-Turkish War of 1897. He was King of Greece from 1913 to 1917 and from 1920 to 1922.
‡ A joint Muslim-Christian assembly including Eleftherios Venizelos was part-elected, part-appointed.

called out from the pavement, "Shaban, you know there's an election tomorrow. Don't forget to use your vote for Captain Kaloyeris."

Shaban Agha was a Turk and a Muslim. As if he would ever vote for the Venizelos crew, the very people who were trying to throw him from his home and country! His response was as dignified and direct as the man himself: "Neighbour," he said, "any Turk who's planning to vote for Venizelos needs their arm cutting off! And the same goes for any Greek that doesn't vote for him!"

Nodding, and in a barely audible voice, Kokoloyannis replied: "You're right, Shaban," and withdrew to his own shop.

My sister and her husband finally left us. With Arif's earnings from ploughing and the money he got for selling their animals and carts, they were able to move to an area closer to the city centre, called Tabyalar, and open a small shop. Sometime later, we followed them, using much the same means; with the money from the sale of our animals and cart, money we had brought with us from the village and our savings put away drop by tiny drop, we were able to move into the city and rent a house in the Veneti Kastana district. It had been seven years since we arrived in Varusi and I was now twenty-one years old. We were to spend over fifteen more years in Chania. The real, great migration didn't happen until the 1920s. That's when we had to swallow the poison of leaving our homeland behind us.

6

Splantzia was famous for its square – a colourful hub of large grocers, dairies, assorted shops and spacious coffeehouses arranged around the huge central fountain. The traders' produce spilled out across the ground and every space was filled by a mass of bobbing heads – some with and some without a fez – both Christians and Muslims. Dyed-in-the-wool Venizelos supporters like Kokoloyannis the cheese trader, anti-Venizelos Greek royalists, Turks hounded from their villages to the city, born-and-bred Chania locals, rich and poor, people with bare feet, people in simple rawhide sandals, people in boots – they were all occupants of this bustling square. But the vast majority of the people among the crowds were Turks. Just as an example, all of the nine large coffeehouses there were run by Turks, but the owner of a shop that sold all kinds of sea fish, from strips of dried salted whiting to sardines, chub mackerel and tuna in brine, was a royalist Greek from the island. Nearby was Kokoloyannis, also from the island, but a supporter of Venizelos, who was leading the campaign to expel us from our homes and country. In the same square, the taverna owner Voleonitis and grocer Manusos both appeared to be neutral but actually supported the Greek king.

Once we had moved to a house inside Chania, I became fed up with the life of a travelling seller wandering the streets with a tray balanced on my head or shoulders. I moved on to selling boiled chestnuts and then endless tiny bowls of the dessert called *Ashure*, "Noah's Pudding". But the time had come to turn my back on such trivial jobs and find something more suited to my maturity. All the time I had spent roving around every place of work and play in the city trying to sell my wares had significantly expanded my horizons and experience. At the Yusuf Kenan Printing House I had learned something of print setting and printing, at Baha Bey's studio I had gleaned a superficial knowledge of photography, and at the many shops I visited time and time again I picked up the basics of the retail trade. That's not to mention the tavernas I went in and out of, evening after evening; there, I learned the rules of nightlife and drinking, which would stand me in good stead later on when I became one of their best customers.

One day, as I was passing in front of Kiri Vladimiros's printing house on the road to Kastel, my mind as usual tangled with ideas and indecisiveness, I heard his deep voice calling after me: "Hassan, come in, my boy. There's something I want to talk to you about."

He was a fair-skinned man with a white beard and huge mouth. His dark bespectacled eyes peered out from heavy lenses clipped in a delicate frame. The stains of printing ink looked even blacker against his fair complexion and hands.

He always wore a black apron to prevent the ink stains ruining his shirts.

"Look, my lad, you've made an impression on me since the first day you came to Chania. Come day or night, winter or summer, you've been up and down with that tray, keeping your family in house and home. And now look at you, you've grown into a man."

"I didn't have any choice, Kiri Vladimiros," I replied. "When you're chased out of your village and even worse, lose your father, you have to work your fingers to the bone whether you like it or not. There've been days, weeks when things went well, and I was so happy and excited that I ran all the way home. But when things didn't go so well, I tried not to think of the words of that folk song that I'm sure you know as well as me: 'I throw straw into the sea, it's heavy and it sinks, Others fire bullets, they fly with open wings!'"

"I know, my boy, I know. Although I can't say I know anything about being thrown from my village, when I was in Constantinople, I learned what it meant to be fatherless. My saviour was my Uncle Stavros. He was a printer and took me under his wing at his huge printing house in Tahtakale in Constantinople. Everything I have today, what I've become, my wealth and the way I think – I owe it all to him."

"So you're from Constantinople, Kiri Vladimiros?"

"Yes, born and bred, Hassanaki. I moved here years ago, thinking I'd be able to earn a better living. It wasn't such a bad decision. Come on, let's go inside and I'll tell you what I want." He led me into the room that he called his "study", immediately to the left of the entrance. Sitting down at the head of a table covered in notebooks and papers, he asked Nikolaki, the errand boy, to bring us a *sumada* syrup with a generous sprinkling of cinnamon.

"Bring over that chair and sit down, my lad," he said, before making me the best proposition I had received in my life. "Hassan, I want to take you on. Altogether there are six people working in this print shop. I want you to take care of the bills for the businesses that use our services. Some of them come here to collect their print orders, so you can give them the bill and take the money in the shop; for the others, I want you to go out and deliver the bill and collect the money from them. You'll bring us new customers and take care of the stocks we need to keep the place running. Basically, you'll be responsible for all our outside business and take care of it for us."

"Of course, I'd be happy to try but…"

"Don't worry at all about wages, Hassan. But we Christians have our weekend holiday on a Sunday, I'm sure you know that. I don't want you to say that you can't work on Fridays. You'll get your weekly wages on Saturday night like the other workers and rest on Sunday, like us. Is that all right?"

I had been looking for a regular job more suited to my age. Now, here with Kiri Vladimiros, I would be protected at least to some degree from the fanatical Greeks, and I would earn enough to be able to look after our household comfortably until another opportunity arose. That's no small thing for someone who's been torn away from their own home and land…

"Kiri Vladimiros, I accept. I'll take care of your customers and I won't let you down."

"I want to give you a book, Hassanaki, as a memory of the day you joined us." He stood up and handed me a bound book from the shelf behind him, saying, "Open it and have a look. It's a Turkish–Greek dictionary that was printed at my uncle's print house. I worked on it too."

I opened it and looked. It was dated 1876. Printed on fine paper, the dictionary had been put together with the help of Maliaka, a teacher from the Imperial Lycée in Galatasaray, Istanbul, and Hafz Refi, who was an Arabic, Persian and Turkish teacher at the same school. It was written in both Hellenic and Arabic alphabets. I was thrilled to receive it. It would be slow going, letter by letter, but, combined with the lessons I had received from Manolis and the village imam, Sherif Efendi, the dictionary would be invaluable to me.

7

My long-suffering mother was elated at seeing her young son taken into regular employment. She prayed and made devotions to the saints. I would now be able to provide a much better living for our household and, if conditions allowed, might bring her a bride and grandchild as well! Of course, she already had a grandchild from my older sister, Nazire, but she said that it was a different feeling to get a grandchild from a son. The murder of my brother, and then losing my father when the mosque was shelled, increased my mother's affection for me and meant she fussed over me even more. Overcome with happiness, she hung on to me for what seemed like an eternity, saying, "My Hassan, my son!"

Around dusk, we wanted to go and pass on the good news to my sister and brother-in-law in Tabyalar, but my mother was apprehensive about going there: "There've been some bad rumours; they say the Greeks have brought trouble into the city. Nothing's going to happen to us, is it?"

"Don't worry," I replied. "I'll be next to you! All these years I've spent on the streets, in and out of the crowds, even after dusk, I've learned a lot about people – the good and the bad. We'll get there, and we'll get back again."

When I arrived in Tabyalar with my mother, covered in her black *abaya*, my brother-in-law was in the middle of closing up the shop. He too was concerned about the rumours and, worried that something might happen to him, he had taken to closing the shop early to give him enough time to get home in the early evening.

Nazire and Arif were thrilled that I had been saved from the life of a street-hawker, but they were also apprehensive. My brother-in-law voiced their fears. "There's just one thing – this man you're talking about is one of the educated Greeks, who can read and write. I hope he's not going to try and make you one of them."

My mother agreed. "I'm happy you've found a job, but it makes me sick to the stomach to think about what Arif said. God forbid!"

Although the joy of landing a decent job had brought with it some anxieties, I trusted myself to remain true to my ancestors. "Thanks to the way you brought me up, I know my traditions and my religion. I know about my Turkish roots. I learned our Qur'an as well. I know more than I don't know. I've learned how they write and I've got to know a lot of people over all the years I've been out and about selling. I've earned my stripes now. It's not that easy to push me around. Come on, all of you, stop worrying!"

Nazire threw her support behind me saying, "You're worrying for nothing. The Hassan I know wouldn't let anyone try to make him something he's not. He knows what he's doing!"

"I know Hassan as well," Arif insisted, "but I'm worried and I need to speak my mind. All of us that escaped here to Chania, we don't get much news from outside, so we don't always notice what's really going on. I'll tell you what I heard yesterday about a massacre in Floria village on the way to Kandanos. Some brigands arrived and told the people there were Greek mobs on the way and that they should come with them to escape to safety. About fifteen Turks believed them and followed them out of the village. The brigands shot them all dead."

After Arif's words, the room seemed to turn as cold as ice; but no one said anything. What can you say in such a hopeless situation? No one mentioned my new job again.

PART TWO

"I saw my fate, upon the rocks,
In the darkness of the valley,
It was dressed in mourning."

Cretan Folk Song

8

The only interruptions to the otherwise calm life of Chania were the sporadic murders of Turks in the city. News of torchings, desecrations and massacres outside the city travelled to the urban population a couple of days after the event, provoking a wave of panic and fear. One of the reasons given for the low number of incidents inside the city was that the Greeks were wary about news of murders reaching the consulates of the great powers in the Halepa district of Chania. Because of this, they intimidated us in other ways, acting on individual grudges rather than executing planned murders, as if to hiss, "I'll show you, you Turkish bastards!"

On days like these, life was drained of any merriment or joy. Some of the savagery was so barbaric that even the Greeks, who had the same blood flowing through their veins, reacted against it. The kidnap of a woman named Havva* caused consternation in some Greek circles. On the way to see her fiancé with her father, she was attacked by Greeks

---

* Havva is the Turkish name for Eve.

on Tahta Bridge. The kidnappers, Deaf Yorgi and his gang, raped Havva for weeks, before taking her off to a monastery to convert her to Christianity. There was no way Havva could defend herself physically against that number of men, but when she resisted their efforts to make her change her religion, they set her free like a living corpse.

It was a long time since I had seen Daggerlad, and in the meantime Kiri Vladimiros became my second guardian. Just as Daggerlad had sworn to be there for me in the case of mortal danger, Kiri Vladimiros extended his protective arm by appreciating my diligence and giving me the benefit of regular employment. Even more important than this was his warmth and sincere care for me. For one thing, whenever this kind of terrible news was doing the rounds, he would do whatever he could, directly or indirectly, to comfort me. The knowledge that I was safe under his protective wing made me feel I could speak openly and pour out my heart to him.

Of the many people working at the printers, there was just one man who was at odds with the brotherly attitude of Kiri Vladimiros: that was the oldest print-setter, Vomvolakis. He was one of those who simply didn't like us Turks and wanted us gone from Crete. He took great pleasure in rattling my nerves. The boss knew what he was like, so whenever he saw him speaking to me or heading in my direction, he would say, "Get on with your job, Vomvolakis! Cut the prattle."

But unable to stop himself sticking the knife in, Vomvolakis would make sure he had his say as he walked away. "There's one less of your lot now, Hassanaki."

When the news about Havva reached Chania, I was in the print house office, preparing the list of bills arising from that day's work. Towards evening, I would work out the bills for the print house and hand over the money from my daily collections to Kiri Vladimiros. That evening, as Vomvolakis came towards the desk where I was making my calculations, I saw Kiri Vladimiros suddenly appear from behind him.

"Come on, my fellow Christian," he began, "leave the man alone."

The sullen-faced print-setter went back to his work and the boss pulled up a chair to sit next to me. Knowing what had happened to Havva, he said, "These incidents are terrible, Hassanaki, there's no doubt about that. They're a blight on humanity. You can't stop them and neither can I. It's really hard to stop the tide of savagery – in fact, it's impossible! After this, your people are going to respond with a murder somewhere else on the island."

"Where will it all end? Are they going to keep on raping and killing like this? Isn't it a tragedy, Kiri Vladimiros?"

"Of course it's a tragedy, my lad. I know it's going to hurt you when I say this, but the murders will carry on until they've succeeded in throwing you all off the island."

"But this is where our ancestors are from. I was thinking about it just the other day and if I'm not mistaken, fifteen generations of Turks have grown up here. If we're honest about it, they – I mean your kinfolk – arrived after us and made it their homeland. All I'm trying to say is that it's our homeland as much as it's theirs. So what's all the fighting about when we were getting along just fine together, like oranges and lemons growing in the same field? After what happened to Havva today, every Turk is miserable! This last incident…"

"Hassanaki, that's the way these things go. There have been a lot of rebellions on this island, for as long as Crete has been Crete. Every one of them has been put down. But this time, this rebellion organised by Venizelos will make Crete part of Greece; in fact, it already has!"

"You're certainly right there, boss," I muttered.

"I learned to see things for what they really are when I was in Tahtakale in Istanbul. We all got on well together there, the Turks and the Greeks. All in all, we were honest with each other and lived with mutual respect."

"So why is it different here, then?"

"Look, Hassanaki, I'm Greek too. I'm a part of the Cretan Greeks, the same race and religion. But unfortunately, we don't all think the same way. I'm all for compassion and enjoying life, without making divisions between people; but others are all for gaining land and expanding their territory in the name of 'homeland'."

"And they're killing people for that? Why are there so many Greeks who are ready to kill people?"

"It's the result of living under the rule of your Turks for hundreds of years. They're sick of it and this is their reaction: violence and killing. Those at the top are trying to make a name for themselves by setting us innocent people against each other. It's always the ordinary people who suffer. If they knew the good things about the Turks like I do, if they read as much as me and saw the reality, they wouldn't behave like such barbarians."

"Absolutely right, boss," I responded, "I haven't wanted to talk about what happened in Baduryana village last week… maybe you heard about it as well but didn't let on; that was another inhuman crime. After the murders by the Captain Bunato gang, Cemal and Mustafa Baduraki panicked and fled the village with their families. They managed to get to the sea and on to a boat but after that no one knows what happened to them. I don't know if they managed to get to Anatolia, or if the sea carried them to the shores of North Africa or if they ended up as fish bait."

"Let's hope they were saved…" sighed Kiri Vladimiros, "You know, I haven't told you about the gangs of the past. The leaders of the previous rebellions – they call them captains – were even more ruthless, more fearless. Furogatos, Skoulakis, Michalis, Orphanoudakis – they were all human butchers! Some of them used to hold the decapitated heads of Turks up by the hair to brag to their friends, letting the blood drip out drop by drop!"

I felt sick to the stomach, "Don't tell me any more, boss. Please…"

"OK, Hassanaki. But in return for me changing the subject, I want to ask you a favour. You know the *kipohorta* your mamma makes? I want a huge tray when she makes the first batch. I don't mean just a tiny taster like last time, I want a huge plate of it – a pot full!"

Vladimiros's wife, Kiriya Evthimiya, was an Istanbulite like him. She knew how to make the special herb and vege-table dishes of our island, but they weren't as delicious as my mother's cooking. On the other hand, when it was the right season, Kiriya Evthimiya's stuffed mackerel was the perfect accompaniment for an evening spent drinking white wine. Not to mention the huge turkey eggs she cooked every spring, breaking a couple of them into a pan of olive oil – our magnificent Cretan olive oil – and sprinkling the yolks with a pinch of dried mint powder. Concerned for her husband's health, she only allowed him one mouthful; the rest was left for me – the young stripling!

Kiri Vladimiros took the list of income and expenses from me, carefully folded it in half and placed it in his pocket with the drachma I had given him. "As always, I'll look at these in the peace of home, and prepare the next day's work schedule. It's Saturday today. Your mamma knows you're coming to eat with us this evening and you'll be late home. So come on, let's go and see what wonderful meze Evthimiya has for us."

Five or six years younger than her husband, Kiriya Evthimiya was an adorable woman. She was constantly smiling, and her short, plump figure darted around the house excitedly when we were all together. As they had no children of their own, they lavished all their love on me. They appreciated my honesty with money, my hard-working nature and good manners, treating me just like a son. Before I came along, they had always employed their own kinsfolk to do the errands and accounts, but everyone had ended up cheating and stealing from them. Within a year of taking me on, I became a regular Saturday night visitor to their home, frequently invited to join them for dinner and wine after work.

For Kiriya Evthimiya, every Saturday was a celebration. Along with Kiri Vladimiros, I would go into the dining room they called *trapezariya* and make myself at home. Everything gleamed, including the face of Evthimiya, who greeted us with a huge smile. The weekend wine sessions were naturally accompanied by fish and meat meze. One fine example was Kiriya Evthimiya's fried calf's liver. She could rustle up a sauce for it in just a few minutes, mixing together vinegar and the herb we called *bibiriye* and the Greeks called *rozmari*. We couldn't help but lick our fingers afterwards. However, there were never any vinegary foods or salads when wine was on the table and, as the sauce contained vinegar, on the Saturdays when liver was served we drank *raki*, some called it *ouzo*, instead of wine. Kiriya Evthimiya made the same sauce to liven up common, cheap fish that wasn't considered a luxury, turning it into a flavoursome treat.

My mother was an exceptional cook of a different sort. Our rich tradition of vegetable and herb dishes stemmed from a life of living from the land. According to my mother, the secret of these dishes lay in knowing how best to use onions. Onions added when raw never gave any taste. She used copious amounts of onions, swirling them in a pan of olive oil until they turned pink. For other types of dishes, she cooked the onions in water, adding oil afterwards. She also used a lot of olive oil. Black pepper, cumin, bay, thyme, garlic, dill, parsley and rosemary were the gems of her kitchen. As alcohol wasn't part of our tradition, she didn't know about making meze, but she was a maestro with hot meals. My taste buds and stomach were always brimming with contentment thanks to the delicious cooking of my mother and Kiriya Evthimiya.

9

It was only during Ramadan that I skipped the Saturday night gatherings at Kiri Vladimiros's house, prohibiting myself from my once-weekly indulgence in alcoholic drink. I might not have prayed regularly, but I always fasted. I always made sure I was home sitting with my mother at the table when it was time to break the fast. Naturally, I was tired when I came home from work during Ramadan. That was why at the beginning, whenever I was able to, I would go to the nearer Sultan's mosque or the Algerian mosque for the evening *Tarawih* prayers. The latter had been named in memory of the Algerian soldiers brought to the island for the conquest of Crete. Later, towards the end of Ramadan, I usually found time to visit the other mosques of Chania. In 1913, after Crete was ceded to Greece, our biggest mosque, the Sultan's mosque, was converted into the Church of Agios Nikolaos and the Waterside and Yusuf Pasha Mosques started to become almost as crowded as the Algerian Mosque.

Just as I said at the start, our Turkish identity and Islam were our greatest pride: everything else was insignificant. The prevalence of mosques in Chania was symbolic for us.

There were plenty that I never had time to go to: Kastel, Ağa Mevlevihane, Kalekapısı and Kumkapı Mosques to mention just a few.

On Fridays during Ramadan, as I didn't want to go too far from work, I used to pray at the Kastel Mosque, which was just up from the fountain. Unlike his wife, Kiri Vladimiros didn't believe in God. Whenever I went to ask leave to go to the mosque, I could see him smiling, not just under his moustache, but with his eyes as well.

"That's fine, Hassanaki," he used to say. He never interfered in anyone's personal business.

I was the only one in the printing house who knew he was an atheist. He used to talk about it at the table on Saturday evenings – things like that were never discussed at work. It would have been over-familiar with the employees, and not only that, but in all likelihood the rumour would have spread like wildfire until it reached the ears of the church, leading to condemnation and social and economic boycott. That would be enough to cause a successful businessman like him, with a family and reputation to uphold, to die of grief.

Ramadan brought an even livelier bustle to the streets of Chania. After evening prayers, Splantzia Square filled with people; it was a place of games that went on until the middle of the night, where people smiled and had fun, hoping to win one of the trays of *baklava* or lamb that were given as prizes. The square, frequented by Turks from all walks of life, was turned into a street festival full of tombolas, Ramadan conjurors, luxury treats and gas lamps that multiplied in honour of the month.

There was a particular atmosphere on each one of our public holidays. The Ramadan holiday was one thing and Eid-al-adha was something else. Visitors coming to the house during Ramadan were offered home-made *baklava* and citrus jams. My mother also made jam from the local fruit, *kitro*, which was sold to Europe even back in those days.

After all the tragedy we had been through, the customs and traditions taught to us by my father held strong, and we tried to get on well with our new neighbours. We were always respectful and friendly. Our relations with the Greeks on our street, apart from the odd few sullen characters, were not bad at all, although we didn't have much to do with each other. At the appropriate time of year, they would wish us well using the Turkish expression, *"iyi bayramlar"* and we would be sure to wish them *"iyi yortular"* in Greek when it was their feast time.

They would give us gifts of eggs, pastries and *koliva*, while we offered *baklava*, pies and sacrificial meat from our slaughtered animals. Our relationships were based on the rules of reciprocation, but the values my father had drummed into us meant that we were always the most selfless. We just wanted to live in peace and contentment in our new home. After being chased from our home, and losing my father and brother, we had no desire to add any more woes.

The day we heard the Greeks were on their way to Anatolia,* we wept in our homes. The Greeks in Chania were

---

* In 1919, after the defeat of the Ottoman Empire in the First World War, Greek forces landed in Izmir encouraged by promises of territorial gain from the western Allies and particularly from British prime minister David Lloyd George.

celebrating as if it were a wedding carnival. For us, it crushed our spirit. Yet what could we do but try to get on with them? We were mortally wounded by the sight of captured Turkish soldiers and officers being brought over as prisoners of war from Anatolia and incarcerated in a camp in Chania. I began to visit to offer consolation, although trying not to make it too public, and whenever our means allowed it, I would take something along for them.

As time passed, the Greek guards on the gate got used to me and didn't mind my visits. I became good friends with an imprisoned lieutenant from Bursa. When he found out he was a few years older than me, he began to see himself as my big brother, taking it as his duty to develop my Turkish. "Hassan, you hardly know any Turkish. It's unbelievable. It's a disgrace!"

"It's not my fault, Kemalettin Bey," I replied. "That's all I could pick up in the village and in Chania."

"Knowing thirty or forty words doesn't count as knowing Turkish. We need to work on it."

"How can we do that?" I asked.

"What about coming over here for an hour on Saturdays before you go to eat at your boss's place? If you can get an hour's leave each week, we'll eventually sort you out."

"All right, but I can't read those Arabic letters. I know how to read the Qur'an, but I really can't write anything."

"If you're patient, you'll learn that too. Let's just make a start and we'll see how it goes."

Kiri Vladimiros was pleased when I told him the news. He said it was essential for me to learn the culture of my ancestors. From now on, every Saturday afternoon, I had leave to learn Turkish. One notebook and one pen were more than enough for us to start our studies. Every lesson, Kemalettin Bey would write ten words in my notebook, then ask me to write them over and over again. It was exasperating for me that he wrote in Arabic letters, but the rules of the lesson were that I had to copy them out. As he was writing, Kemalettin Bey said the words out loud, explained the meanings and made me repeat each one. He also pronounced each letter of the word individually as he was writing it.

I struggled writing the words out in huge Arabic letters and trying to memorise them. To be more precise, I was totally disheartened and eventually made a suggestion to Kemalettin Bey: "Every day, I write Greek. That's how I do the company accounts. Don't you think I'd learn better and more quickly if I wrote down what you teach me in the letters I'm used to – in Greek letters?"

He paused, not quite comprehending my words.

"It's just that I was telling Kiri Vladimiros how difficult it was for me with the Arabic letters and he said there are Greeks living in the middle of Anatolia, the *Karamanlides*, who speak Turkish but write in Greek letters – completely opposite to the Cretan Turks. I mean, they write and speak Turkish using the Greek alphabet."

"Let me see you write down a few examples and hear you read them," said Kemalettin Bey.

He pronounced some completely new Turkish words, enunciating them slowly as I wrote them down. After I managed to write down the syllables, he asked me to read the words out and was pleasantly surprised to hear the words trip off my tongue. "Hassan, with this new method I'll be able to teach you more than I expected at the beginning. Come on, let's get to work!"

As the weeks passed, my Turkish vocabulary expanded. Being an Istanbulite himself, Kiri Vladimiros oversaw what I had learned after every lesson, asking me to read out what I had written, then listening out to correct any omissions or mistakes. Kemalettin Bey, who monitored my progress by making me repeat the previous week's lesson, was pleased with how much I had learned. His work was all the more successful due to the additional help of Kiri Vladimiros explaining the meanings of the Turkish words to me in Greek. Really, I had two Turkish teachers – one direct and one indirect. In time, starting off with simple expressions, I was able to construct whole sentences of my own.

10

Kiri Vladimiros was a person brimming with humanity, of the kind that didn't stop him criticising his own people when necessary, and didn't prevent him seeing both the good and the bad in them. After all, he had grown up in the Ottoman capital, where his profession as a printer had encouraged him to read and develop his own judgement. His ideas were shaped by the common decency necessary for communal co-existence. Even now, years later, as I write this and think of the things I've seen in some of the people from Central Anatolia who like us have come and settled here, I realise he was a special person who genuinely knew what he was talking about.

One Saturday evening, as we were eating and drinking around the large table in his house, I asked him, "Have your Greeks always been ruled by our Turks?"

"That's a good question, Hassanaki," mused Kiri Vladimiros. "Until your Turks came this way from Central Asia, the Greeks were spreading their wings unchecked. The people at the top know these things, but not ordinary Greeks –

they think it was only the Turks who came from somewhere else and that's why they attack them."

"Really, is it true?"

"Really, Hassanaki. The Greeks have some crimes to answer for going back to before your ancestors arrived, never mind what they're doing to you now. Before the Ottomans were even dots on the horizon, my kinsfolk passed through Asia Minor – I mean Anatolia – and to the north of Afghanistan, through Samarkand and Kabul to China. On the way they declared some places Greek states. I know the names are strange to you because you haven't studied geography, but they're real. Remind me on Monday and I'll show them to you on the world atlas at the print house."

"It's unbelievable!"

"Believe it, my lad! Believe it! My ancestors were the chief conquerors, and not just in Asia and Asia Minor – they spread along the whole of the Mediterranean. They sent in the priests and converted a lot of people to Christianity. I don't want to confuse you too much with all this, so I'll just say that they spread across Asia, Africa and the whole of Europe. It carried on until the Europeans got sick of it and stopped us in our tracks. Afterwards, your Turks came from Central Asia and started driving us out, squeezing us into a smaller space. That's what's behind this fight now: the Greeks being shrunk into a smaller space after all that expansion. Unfortunately for my people, the Turks were warriors."

"I can hardly believe what you're saying."

"In the future, when you've had more chance to read and open your eyes, you'll understand the truth in what

I'm saying. Don't let the murders here frighten you. We're in the death throes of Greek expansionism. We've got the Europeans on one side and your people from Central Asia on the other, taking our swords from us and breaking them in two. If you think about it, you can see that we Greeks have become trading people. When we were forced to slow down on all sides, we turned to trade."

"You say, 'Don't be afraid,' but how can I not be afraid? They murdered the two people who were the backbone of our family, they drove us from our land, our home!"

Kiri Vladimiros took a few more of the stuffed squash flowers that my mother had made for me to bring and placed them on his plate. "These taste so good – good enough to make a man forget to drink his wine."

After sipping a mouthful of wine, he placed one of the stuffed flowers in his mouth and began to chew.

"Let me repeat myself to make sure you understand what I'm saying. My people are floundering in the water and as the ripples spread out, they cause the kind of tragedies that happened to you. Just like I said, the Greeks were expanding, and everything was going well. Then along came the newcomers and pushed us out, as far as this island. Now we're in a battle over the last place we were chased to. Do you see what I mean?"

We were interrupted by the smiling face of Kiriya Evthimiya, "That's enough explaining for now, Vladimiros. You've talked so much, Hassanaki looks thunderstruck. Talk about something a bit lighter. Try a bit of this chard pie, both of you."

11

My relationship with the glamorous Hüsnüye, the sister-in-law of Blind Rahmi, began on the day my family bought a house in Chania. When we put together the money left from my wages at the print house, the money saved from my street sales and what remained from the things we had brought from the village, we were able to buy the house we had been renting in Veneti Kastana. It was lucky for me that my mother was such an industrious and thrifty person. I was thirteen years old when we were hounded from the village and by the time we bought the house in the city I was twenty-one. These days, I wore a fez on my head. I had to make sure I was smartly dressed and well turned out now I was working for a Christian and responsible for the print house's external business. I gradually got used to taking extra care over my appearance and eventually took great pleasure in it.

It was Hüsnüye who gave me the name Aynakis, meaning "little mirror". The label stuck and became my nickname for ever after. It was a fact that the way I dressed attracted attention from women – both Greeks and Turkish – and I loved it.

I had certainly been awoken by seeing my big brother fooling around with the widow Photini next door in our village.

At that time, up until I got together with Hüsnüye, I was a regular visitor to a Greek woman who received men at her house in the suburbs of Chania. She satisfied my physical needs although I knew that I also longed for something deeper. I knew that sleeping with a woman with no mutual flirtation, no laughing together or kissing was nothing more than a discharge of energy...

With Hüsnüye, I experienced absolute passion and togetherness. Her brother-in-law worked in Floru's coffeehouse in Splantzia and despite having perfect eyesight was for some reason called Blind Rahmi. It was another nickname, like Aynakis, and I wasn't sure if it was because he was unaware what his sister-in-law got up to, or for some other reason. One day, as I was passing in front of Floru's coffeehouse, I heard his voice call out from the stove at the back of the café.

"Aynakis! Good day to you!"

I turned and entered the café. "Hey," I said, "I guess it's me you want to talk to, but why are you calling me Aynakis?"

He leaned over, closer to my ear.

"That's what my sister-in-law, Hüsnüye, calls you. I know your name is Hassanakis."

"So you mean that I have a name that I don't know, Aynakis, thanks to your sister-in-law, who I also don't know?"

Rahmi smiled. "So it seems! It's not such a bad name..."

He explained why he had called me over. His sister-in-law needed some help with an official problem and he wondered if I could sort it out. He seemed to think I would be able to do it because it was straightforward and, in any case, Vladimiros would be able to give me some advice about it. He described the location of her house so I could go and get some more details. He didn't neglect to say that I would be paid for my trouble.

The next morning, as I set off with my daily list of jobs for the print house, I considered whether or not I should go to the house of the renowned, glamorous Hüsnüye at this time of the morning. In the end, I decided to go. It would be a thrill to see a woman famous for her looks dressed in her casual house clothes first thing in the morning. And who knows what might happen, maybe... I woke up from my fantasy and gave myself a good talking to. "Stop it," I told myself, "People like that have better things to do than hang around for people like you." Nevertheless, she had found time to give me a special nickname... Surely that meant something?

With my mind lost in all these thoughts, I finally found Hüsnüye's house and knocked on the door at 9 a.m. An elderly woman opened the door. I told her I had been sent by Blind Rahmi and gave my name. After keeping me waiting on the street so long that I was starting to get irritated, she invited me in and signalled for me to sit down and wait on the bench just by the entrance. I had been sitting there for a while when a woman appeared at the head of the stairway leading to the upper floor. She stopped for a moment and looked down at me. She was a curvaceous woman, but the top and bottom halves of her body tapered to a point so finely as to give the impression of two separate triangles; in the middle, her delicate waist added an alluring elegance to her ample body. She was fair-skinned, had long, raven hair in copious ring curls and wore make-up. She came down the stairs and casually sat down on the other end of the bench. Her eyes were as black as her hair.

"Hassan Efendi," she began, "I spoke to my brother-in-law about you three days ago. He told me he saw you yesterday, so I was expecting you today. Did he at least tell you it was me who gave you the name Aynakis?"

"Yes, he told me to come and see you and he also told me about the name."

Her dark eyes were looking straight into mine. "We can have a coffee together, can't we?"

Without waiting for my answer, she asked the other woman to make two coffees. Then she began to explain her problem. There had been an inheritance from her father, which had been split equally between her and another daughter, Rahmi's wife. Regrettably, instead of taking care of their share of the money and making something of it, her sister and brother-in-law had burnt through it in no time, which meant that Rahmi now had to work on a coffee stove. As for her, I don't know how she managed it, but she didn't just look after her own share, she used her enterprising female nature to turn it into a good income, enough to stand on her own two feet. Recently, however, a Greek had turned up, claiming to have some papers that showed he was the true owner of a shop that Hüsnüye was renting out. She wanted me to take care of the matter on her behalf until her name was cleared.

Compared to Mahmut's lover, Photini, and the woman in the suburbs of Chania who had given me my first experiences, this woman had a different air about her. This was something else. I had a feeling of being pulled towards a precipice by her eyes, a bewildering, intoxicating air of arousal. The excitement of uncertainty. As she sipped coffee and explained the story, she was also slowly moving nearer to me, at times touching or even holding on to my arm as she tried to emphasise a certain point she was making. Something in her manner and the way she spoke filled me with an urge to caress her face and put my arms round her delicate waist.

I passed on the information she had given me to Kiri Vladimiros to ask for his help in figuring out what I should do. He sat at the table and wrote a petition in the name of Hüsnüye, telling me to take it back to her the next morning to get her seal. Then I was to take it to an official, called Stamatakis, who worked in the local administration, and make sure to pass on his best wishes at the same time. Stamatakis would be able to resolve the matter, but Kiri Vladimiros advised me to take along five *oka* of the local cheese called *malaka* that had just been made, together with a demijohn of good wine.

In the morning, I went back to Hüsnüye's house to read her the petition and get her seal. I told her the recommended bribes and she agreed to all of them. Afterwards, I headed for the local government offices, where I found Stamatakis straightaway. I whispered into his ear what Vladimiros had told me and his face lit up immediately on hearing the name of his old friend. He read the petition carefully, before saying, "What Kiri Vladimiros has written here is absolutely correct. You can assure him the subject is closed."

While sorting this out, to make sure the print house daily affairs didn't fall behind schedule, I had been dropping into Hüsnüye's in the morning on my way out after picking up the list of tasks from the office. The next morning, I calculated the cost of the cheese and wine and knocked on her door once again. I reported back on the events of the previous day: that the petition written in her name had been accepted, that the Greek would no longer be able to interfere in the shop and that there was nothing more she needed to worry about on that front. I also told her the costs that had been incurred from the wine, cheese and two porters to carry it all. This morning, the elderly woman wasn't around and Hüsnüye's invitation to coffee felt different, somehow more enticing. "Hatice isn't here," she began, "You'll join me for something sweet followed by a coffee made by my own fair hand, won't you?"

She presented me with the classic offering of Cretan hospitality, marmalade accompanied by a glass of water, then went into the kitchen to prepare the coffee. After a short time, I got up and went towards the kitchen, driven by my desire to hear more of the husky, guttural voice that I found so attractive. I wanted to feel her next to me. I had to know how she felt. There was something about this woman that had turned my head upside down for the last three days, that made me forget the fear and panic all around me and just think about wanting her. The work I had done for her and my payment were a million miles from my thoughts.

Hearing my timid footsteps behind her, she turned, making me stop in my tracks before I was near enough to touch her. "I would have brought your coffee. You didn't need to come."

Making no attempt to hide my desire, I looked into her eyes, overwhelmed with the feeling of being pulled into the darkness of a bottomless well. "I wanted to get closer to you and hear your voice again."

"Hatice could come back at any moment… We'll be a disgrace!"

There was something flimsy about her rejection – something that made me doubt its sincerity. The sequence of recent events whirled through my head, starting from giving me, a stranger, a nickname, then telling me all her problems virtually on the doorstep, inviting me inside, and brushing against my hand and arm with every second sentence. And as if that wasn't enough… Weren't those sultry looks she gave me? And why send Hatice away on an errand at the very time she knew I was coming… only to threaten me with Hatice to keep me in my place? It made no sense.

Placing my two hands on her slender waist, I pulled her towards me and planted a lingering kiss on her cheek at the edge of her mouth. She was stunned into silence, and collapsing into the chair next to the table, began to take deep gulps of air. Her face, framed with long curls, had gone bright red and her nostrils widened. She was taller and bigger than me and I wondered how I had managed to spirit my mouth on to hers unless she had instinctively leaned down towards me when she felt my hands on her waist – there was no other explanation for it. Emboldened by her red face and the loosening of her body, this time I kissed her on the lips.

The kiss gave way to a storm of passion. Our bodies were entwined, and as we lost ourselves in the hungry kisses, I felt her take control of me. Now it was she who was leading the way. It seemed clear that the worry of being discovered by Hatice had been just a yarn. She was doing things to me that I had never experienced or felt when I was with the Greek woman on the outskirts of town. When I could take it no more, she fell back on to the wicker chair, pulling me down between her open legs. And there, with her cries reverberating around the kitchen walls, the storm abated. As she leaned back on the chair, her smooth lily-white legs wide apart, she tried to cover herself with her hands.

12

Taking care of the print house nitty-gritty meant that I got to learn about all shades of Chania life. So when Kiri Vladimiros began to cut down on his alcohol drinking due to his age and the heat, particularly in the summer, I was happy to hang out at the tavernas with others of my age in the week, and sometimes on Saturdays as well after I had taken my leave from Kiri Vladimiros and his wife. The print house was a school to me in many ways: firstly, it introduced me to the more serious world of commerce, very different to the life of a street seller; secondly, it opened my mind; and lastly, it taught me how to behave with different people and get things done. Even better, I was now making a comfortable living. But best of all these positives was meeting the magnificent Hüsnüye.

Hüsnüye was as warm as she was beautiful. But that was something that only those close to her could have known. The precious secrets of her private world, her sexual warmth and finesse were things that could only be known by the few people like me that she had taken into her arms. People looking at her from the outside remarked on her beauty, while talking maliciously behind her back, but that was it. They knew nothing of her former life in Kumkapı,* the poor district of Chania inhabited by seafarers, of her North African roots, or of her expertise in love; nothing of the exquisite way she prepared a table of meze to accompany drinking, nor how perfect she was as a drinking companion, never losing her impeccable manners.

Knowing only too well what poverty was, Hüsnüye had skilfully managed to make a living from her portion of the money left to her from her seafaring father's lifetime of struggle to look after his daughters. Unlike her sister and brother-in-law, she had used her share with the utmost care and protected what she had. I often wondered about her sexual passion and where she had learned her skills. Now and again, when I felt it was appropriate, I asked her, but she couldn't be made to talk.

"It's in my blood," she would say. "It's part of who I am."

Then, as if to verify her answer, she would immediately start again, leaving no space for further discussion.

She saw me two or three times a week. It was essential for me to be there at exactly the time she stated, down to the minute. I guessed that she had worked out the times according to the movements of her neighbours and anyone else that might be around. Her maid, Hatice, was never there when I went. It was as if the ground had opened and swallowed

---

* In the mid-nineteenth century Kumkapı, on the eastern edge of Chania was a Bedouin village home to 2000-3000 North African slaves and immigrants that mainly worked in the port.

her up every time. The only sounds that broke the silence of the house were Hüsnüye's screams. The noises and gasps she made as her pleasure peaked were like the sounds of someone being strangled. I remember on many occasions worrying that the neighbours would hear, and trying to muffle her screams with the palms of my hands. As well as giving me great pleasure, my relationship with Hüsnüye also educated me about women, standing me in good stead for my later life. After Hüsnüye, my experience in that area attracted four more women, just one of whom was Greek. That's not including the woman I married after I was forced to come to Ayvalık in Turkey in 1923.

Having a job that allowed me to earn a good living, passing time with the friends I made at the tavernas, enjoying a close friendship with my boss and my continuing relationship with Hüsnüye to some degree shielded me from the latest vile acts of those Greeks who wanted to terrorise us into leaving the island. Or perhaps it would be more accurate to say that the atmosphere of panic that followed these incidents had less of an effect on me, in spite of the fact that there were seemingly no limits to what they would do: snatching off a Turk's fez in the street and ripping it to shreds, shouting the most obscene curses and insults against Islam and all things Turkish and calling out to animals like donkeys, dogs and cats using Turkish names. It became commonplace for stones to be thrown at the muezzin when he was reading the call to prayer, and they created a climate of terror by thundering on the doors of Muslims. The remorseless intimidation in its numerous forms was intensifying as they took out their frustrations and injustices on us, vandalising our olive groves and fields, forcing wine down people's throats during Ramadan or making them cross themselves like Christians. Our old people, with their white hair and crooked backs, who no longer had the strength to defend themselves, were attacked in the streets. Local Turks working in government offices were sacked. Our people were murdered and the murderers never found, or if they were found, they were more often than not acquitted; and of those who were convicted, most were out of prison after a few months. Countless, relentless, inhuman acts that wore us down and dragged us towards rebellion.

One evening when I had the chance to drop in at Voleonitis's tavern in Palea Agora, I brought the topic up with my friends Badoyan Mustafa and Grand Mehmed. I wished I hadn't! They became hysterical with despair, throwing down one glass of wine after the other. The workers at the print house constantly fed me with news, some because they liked me and some, like Vomvolakis, because they hated me. But there was bad news from every side. The callousness of two-faced politicians, driven purely by their own interests, was proved to me by a story I heard from Kemalettin, the Turkish officer who had been brought to the prisoner of war camp from Anatolia. Venizelos, the latest ringleader of the bloody uprising intended to throw us from our homeland, had a close accomplice called Mihalis Matrakis, who was combing every inch of the Aegean spreading propaganda: "We've lived under your oppression for hundreds of years, but now the fight is over, and we are the winners. From now on we'll live together under equal conditions. Don't be alarmed. Don't try to resist because the great powers are on our side."

Do you know the most hurtful thing about this? It was the fact that this propaganda was directed at us, the Turks who had been fleeing the oppression and massacres of the island Greeks for so many years. Badoyan Mustafa, who as a caretaker at Darmar Ibrahim's farm in Varusi had, just a week ago, witnessed the full horror of a violent attack on it, was incredulous. "That must be about as low and shameless as you can get," he muttered. "They've been hacking people up and crushing them until they squeal for twenty-five or thirty years now! When did we Turks ever do that to them?"

Grand Mehmed was a bee keeper and now had the miserable task of working out where to hide his beehives from Greek brigands. "They're nearly all the same, all crooks," he said. "They wind up the other Christians to set them against the Turks."

I remembered something Kemalettin had told me and shared it with them.

"Kemalettin said they're making all these speeches to the Turks on the Anatolian coast to deter them from banding together to form a resistance. They know they couldn't stand up to a determined force of united Turks."

The taverna owner, Voleonitis, was a smart man and one of the compassionate Greeks. He was like my boss in many ways. His taverna was a place where we could comfortably discuss any of our concerns and it seemed to attract other mature, like-minded people. There was nowhere I felt happier. Thanks to Voleonitis and the other relaxed customers like him, I felt as comfortable in the tavern as I did at the Saturday night gatherings at the home of Vladimiros. On our island, with its unknown future, Voleonitis's tavern was one of the few places where you could sit and enjoy a few drinks in safety.

There were a few other places our group of friends was able to meet. There was Pavli's taverna, Nuri's taverna in the district called Algiers Point, and our most luxurious haunt, the Renieri. Amongst ourselves, we called the taverna in Algiers Point Nuri's Taverna, although its real name was "Children of War". It was a fitting name for our generation, who were being alienated from our homes and our homeland. The civil war had driven us all the way to the edges of the sea and left us there. Our families had been decimated in one way or another. What struggles lay ahead of us? We had no way of knowing. So it was quite natural that on some nights, as we sat together at Nuri's place, facing into the darkness of our futures, we would raise our glasses and loudly toast, "To us, to the children of war!"

It was only the information I received from Kiri Vladimiros and my teacher, Kemalettin Bey, that stopped me panicking at all the miserable news and ominous developments. Being able to interpret events for myself in some way helped me to maintain a level of contentment in life. I had my compassionate employer on one side and a teacher from my motherland on the other: one a rare benevolent soul despite being a Christian, and the other a victim of war like me. Kemalettin Bey and I had both experienced the atrocities committed by Greeks and both of our futures were dim. Vladimiros thought he would make me feel better by repeating that it was all being orchestrated by those at the top, that the killing and expulsion of ordinary people from their homeland, leaving them destitute and starving, was all a necessary part of their expansion games.

"This battle for territory started with my ancestors," he used to say. "When your Turks arrived from the East, we scarpered and shrank. Now my people have got the foreign powers behind them and are starting to chase yours back. Where it's all going to end, I don't know. Of course, there'll come a time when there's a backlash against their games, and next time, it will be your side chasing and mine fleeing. Whether it's Turks or Greeks, the ones who suffer, the ones who are crushed, are always the people, just the ordinary folk. If it wasn't for the people in power constantly devising these diversions to feather their own nests, all of us, the ordinary people, we'd get along just fine – either living side by side or all jumbled up together. But they won't leave us alone, my lad, they'll never stop setting us against each other. You need to remember that well. You won't be able to stay with me for ever. Who knows – maybe they'll send you all to Anatolia…"

His last words sent me into a panic. I couldn't imagine leaving my Chania, my Crete, the place where I was born and bred. Despite all the pain we had gone through, I was just starting to make something of life. Anatolia might have been my spiritual homeland, but it was an unknown place to me. My real homeland was Crete.

"Don't say that, boss, you're scaring me!"

"I don't want to scare you. I'm just saying what's happened so far, and what might happen in the future. You're like family to us, why would we want you to go? But it's a possibility – quite a strong possibility. Don't you think I'd want you to stay here in Crete, in Chania, even if you didn't work for me?"

"Right now, when I'm able to enjoy a comfortable life for the first time, I can't imagine leaving our island. When it comes to leaving you, that wouldn't even cross my mind unless there was a better-paid job where I was more my own boss. But even if a job like that came up, I still wouldn't leave without talking to you about it. There's no way I would go unless you agreed to it."

13

It had been about a month since the brief but emotional conversation with Vladimiros that had upset both of us. One Saturday evening, I genially declined the usual evening invitation and, with the old couple's blessing, went off to Pavli's taverna. The husband and wife were sympathetic to my reasons for occasionally missing their Saturday evening gatherings. Kiriya Evthimiya said, "You're young. Your mother's old and we're old too. You can't be expected to hang around with old people all the time. At your age, of course you have all kinds of friends to pass time with."

When she said "all kinds of friends", she actually meant Hüsnüye, who they had an inkling I was seeing. However, they were far too polite to say any more than that on the subject. In fact, even as she obliquely referred to it, Kiriya Evthimiya flushed as red as a pomegranate and chuckled.

On a few occasions, as I passed Alyot's café in Splantzia Square, I had noticed the curtains in the house above it moving slightly apart and seen a woman's face looking at me. When I caught her eye, the curtains snapped closed again.

Curiosity about the identity of the woman eventually got the better of me, and after a few inquiries, I found out she was a quite well-to-do woman called Maria who bought and sold houses, shops, orchards, fields and other types of real estate. I was intrigued that a woman could be in that line of business and able to act as a broker at the time, in the 1920s. Working as a street salesman, dealing with the print house external affairs and acting as an intermediary for Hüsnüye had suited me well enough to make me realise that a sedentary job wouldn't suit me. All these experiences had infused me with an ambition to get into the kind of business that I had learned was called brokering. It began to occupy my thoughts nearly all the time, but how could I get off the ground with it?

That evening, I took the long way round to Pavli's taverna, taking me past Alyot's café. This time when I looked up, the woman I had become accustomed to seeing there opened the curtains wide and beckoned with her hand for me to come up. The entrance to the house on the top floor of the café was on a side street. I walked briskly round the corner and knocked on the door. It opened immediately. I heard a woman's voice coming from the top of a steep stairway behind the door. There was no one there who could have opened it. I looked carefully and in the dull light of the gas lamp on the top landing, I could make out a cord running along the wall all the way down to the door. So that's how it had been opened! A woman's voice called down; I presumed it was the woman at the window: "Kiri Hassanaki. Can you come to the office of Varuchakis the lawyer tomorrow after lunch? I want to talk to you about some business."

I was both astonished and excited. A woman I had never met, and about whom I knew nothing apart from the sketchy information about her business affairs, wanted to talk to me about business.

"With great pleasure, Madam," I replied, and bidding her good night, I left. I was so distracted by my thoughts that I don't remember if I even closed the door. I continued on my way to Pavli's taverna, my head still whirring with excitement.

That evening, Ahmet Agha, who was an assistant to the Italian consul, had joined our group of friends. He was a tall, wiry character, fond of good food and white wine. When I say he had a fondness for white wine – it was so much so that he even broke the rules to drink it with meals that were supposed to be accompanied by red wine. There were rumours that he was sleeping with the consul's wife and, naturally, from time to time the subject came up in our banter. "It looks like the Senora's looking after you well. But surely when you're with her you don't drink white wine with pasta?"

He never gave anything away and simply smiled. Everyone had their own interpretation of his smile; some saw it as a yes and some as conclusive evidence that he was having us on. It was from Ahmet Agha that we got much of our information about what was happening on the island and with the British, Greek, Italian and French occupations of the motherland. It was more than enough for him to just keep his ear to the ground at the consulate, and two or three days later, the news was delivered to us in either Pavli's tavern or Nuri's. Ahmet Agha told us that someone called Kemal Pasha* was

---

* Mustafa Kemal Atatürk: Leader of the Turkish War of Independence 1919–1923 and founder of modern Turkey.

organising an army in Anatolia and that the occupying powers were getting worried about it.

As far as we could work out, the foreign consulates in Chania thought that this Pasha's actions in ignoring the Istanbul government and making his name in Anatolia would be a huge obstacle to them handing the Greeks the fertile band of Anatolia along the Aegean coast. That was their main concern. According to the consulates, this Mustafa Kemal was undefeated in any of the battles he had commanded. And if he was successful this time, the Greeks would be in dire straits.

Badoyan Mustafa and Grand Mehmed were rural people, whereas Ahmet Agha was used to the city due to his job. They had different experiences and viewpoints, but they were all honest people; the kind of Turks who were always looking out for you and were sincere in their offers of help. They were the truest friends I had known since Daggerlad. But Daggerlad was someone who met harshness with harshness and could kill a man without batting an eyelid, while Badoyan and Grand were the complete opposite, always seeking a middle road with talk and debate. Their opinions were always based on compassion and they completely opposed the bloodletting and destruction of life. When it came to humanity, they were the Turkish counterparts of Kiri Vladimiros.

Our group was normally eight people, but that evening I was with just three of my close friends, making it easier to bring up the subject of the Greek woman. Badoyan Mustafa spoke with the typical caution of rural people. "Don't make any rash decisions. Does she want you as a partner or a labourer? And what are the conditions, we don't know anything yet!"

Grand Mehmed the beekeeper wasn't short of cautionary advice either. "Whatever she proposes, drive a hard bargain and make sure it's set in stone. If it turns out to be a bad deal, just think how sorry you'll be to lose the nice job you've got now. Don't forget that."

Ahmet Agha had the most positive take on the possible outcomes of this surprise development: "Don't listen to these two," he began. "You need to take a leap of faith. You've got family responsibilities. You need to help out your sister's family and get married yourself. If you accept whatever this madame offers, then make sure you part ways with Kiri Vladimiros on good terms, without offending him, and don't neglect him and Kiriya Evthimiya afterwards. Make them happy by dropping in on them now and again. It's not just a wage that he gives you, he gives you lessons in life as well. He treats you like a son and opens his door to you every week. Not just that, but he knows what he's talking about when it comes to politics and war. His words are priceless. The great Italian consul isn't half as clever as him, I swear. He's a real human being. You'd struggle to find another like him on this huge island. You're really lucky to have a boss like him, Hassan. Never forget it."

Ahmet Agha's hazel eyes were impassioned, and his long arms gesticulated as if to reinforce the meaning of his words. Badoyan and Grand, on the other hand, spoke with the calm born of a life in the countryside. The taverna owner, Pavli, had been watching from the counter and his curiosity had been piqued, particularly by Ahmet's animated hands and arms.

"Hey, boys, what's up with the consul's man?"

"Nothing, nothing. It's something personal. It's not important."

Badoyan, in his typical slow manner, delivered a final pragmatic comment. "Anyway, we're all talking hot air at the moment. We've had a whole discussion without knowing what the woman's going to say or why she wants to see you. You'll find out tomorrow when you see her and then we can talk more. Let's change the subject and enjoy ourselves."

We ordered some of Pavli's delicious fried liver and our evening moved on. Many years later, in the months following the great migration that robbed us of our homeland, we would come across this same fried liver in our Ayvalık, our place of exile; what else could Ahmet Agha do when he got to Ayvalık? There was no Italian consulate he could call on, introducing himself as the man from the consulate in Crete looking for a new job. Instead he brought to Ayvalık the drinking and meze culture of Chania that he had keenly pursued as a customer, but this time pursuing it from the other side of the counter, as a taverna keeper in the Dereboyu district of the town.

The following day after lunch, I took my leave of the print house for an hour and dashed to the office of the lawyer, Varuchakis. Arriving at the door, I dusted myself down and straightened my fez before knocking and entering. At the head of a broad table was a strapping, swarthy man whose huge moustache twirled upwards at the ends, like the German Emperor's. The collar of his shirt bristled skywards like his moustache and he wore a necktie. Sitting across the table from him was a woman dressed in black and wearing a hat. Her left arm rested on the table and her face was turned towards me. I searched for similarities to the face I had glimpsed in the window – was it her or not? Yes, it was her; it must be. The man motioned towards a wicker chair, saying, "Welcome, please sit down." Looking at the woman, he continued, "Should I explain, or would you like to?"

The woman took her eyes off me and turned to the man.

"No, you explain. That would be better."

Then they both turned to look at me.

14

Weighing up Madam Maria's proposition gave me a head-ache, albeit only for a short while. I had a tough job convincing my mother, sister, brother-in-law, Kiri Vladimiros, Kiriya Evthimiya and even my Turkish teacher, Kemalettin Bey. I spent days and nights persuading everyone that it was a genuine offer, especially Hüsnüye. Distressed by the idea that I might take up with Madam Maria, she wept and lamented, while almost tearing me to pieces with her nails. Although I assured her that Madam Maria was a very serious person, and that I hadn't entertained such a thought even for one minute, she continued to sulk and cry. But every argument ended the way she wanted, in intense, stormy passion.

My mother, sister and brother-in-law, Arif, were concerned about whether they would go hungry if I walked away from my current steady, secure job. The income from Arif's small shop wasn't quite enough for them to make a living so they needed my support from time to time. One reason for my mother's unhappiness about this new job was her desire to get me married off. How could she find me a wife if I didn't earn any money and had offended Kiri Vladimiros to boot?

Kemalettin, who was still being held as a prisoner of war, saw things differently. He considered it as the last but one step along the way to being my own boss and earning more money. For that reason, I should make the most of the opportunity and not let it slip from my hands. In his opinion, I shouldn't drag things out too long before accepting the job as I might miss out on the opportunity altogether. He thought it would be to my own detriment if I did anything else.

Kiriya Evthimiya and the white-haired Kiri Vladimiros shared their thoughts one evening as we sat around another elaborately prepared meal. Kiriya Evthimiya's cheery and affectionate character made it seem natural for me to call her Aunt. Just like Aunt Evangeliki, the mother of Manolis my teacher, she was always trying to ply me with food. My mother used to say, "They'll all be saints. Don't take any notice of the fact that they're Christians. They've got as much of a place up in God's kingdom as Muslims like us!"

According to her beliefs, we Muslims were destined for heaven. Any Christians who opened their arms to help rather than persecute us would be able to join us there. She was a fervent believer who never questioned the reasons why we Muslims, God's beloved servants, were being persecuted and pillaged. The table that evening was decked with a magnificent spread; Kiriya Evthimiya and Kiri Vladimiros wanted to make sure that the evening on which we were to discuss parting ways would be a lavish one. All the meze and other dishes had been prepared from seafood. That evening, Aunt

Evthimiya proved even more than usual her supremacy at the art of meze. Naturally, in the middle of the table was a fine white wine, especially selected to complement the meze.

It was Kiriya Evthimiya who broached the topic before her husband, revealing their sadness at the thought of no longer seeing me every Saturday evening. "We've got used to you being around, as if you were our own son – a son that works somewhere far away during the week and only comes home on Saturdays."

It struck me that the perpetual smile on her face seemed somehow subdued, that she hadn't been looking at me as she spoke, but hung her head down towards her plate.

Raising the first glass, Kiri Vladimiros said, "Don't be upset. Let's wish that this new job brings happiness and makes Hassanaki a wealthy man. Come on, lad, raise your glass." I told them how I had been totally preoccupied since receiving Madame Maria's offer and that I couldn't find a way out of my dilemma. In terms of money, Madam Maria's offer was more than satisfactory. I was to get half of the money we earned from every brokering deal and a quarter of any profit we made on properties that she bought and renovated before they were sold. Obviously as she had invested all the capital, she would get the lion's share. There was nothing I could object to in relation to this aspect of the job, because she had set up the business and would also provide all the investment necessary.

Kiri Vladimiros said, "I understand all of it, Hassanaki: that you want to be more independent, earn more money – it's just that I can't imagine life without our Hassanaki, our substitute son. I don't know if you realise how much pleasure and purpose you've brought into our lives. In fact, I might as well tell you now, Evthimiya and I talked a lot about adopting you and even looked into it. But it was impossible with you being a Muslim and us Christians, and on top of that, our communities becoming sworn enemies… murdering each other mercilessly in cold blood. Impossible. In the eyes of society, you're a Turk or a Mohammedan and we are Greeks or Christians. I'm sure you know what I'm saying. We don't have children and we wanted you to have our property, the print house and whatever bit of money we leave behind when we pass away, but we didn't want to separate you from your mother and family. You can see it as our wish to reward good people, but I don't want to put it like that, because being a good person is a basic condition for everyone who calls themselves human. So, I'd rather refer to it as support than reward."

'Thank you, you are both such caring people," I said. "But please, don't talk like that, you're bringing tears to my eyes."

Before I had even finished the sentence, Aunt Evthimiya got to her feet and hurried into the kitchen, sobbing. I didn't know what to do. I looked at Kiri Vladimiros. His eyes had misted over. Then, he pulled himself together and cleared his throat before calling out towards the kitchen, "Come on, Evthimiya, come back. You're upsetting both of us. It's not as if he's leaving Chania, he'll still be here. Whenever he wants to see us he'll come and visit and taste your meze. And when we're missing him, we'll call him over. If he has any problems, we'll be there for him. If we need any help he'll come running. Let's leave him to do what he wants – he's a young man."

Kiriya Evthimiya returned, dabbing her eyes with a white handkerchief. Her nose was as pink as a radish.

"Hassanaki, my son, you won't forget us, will you?"

"How could I ever forget? Kiri Vladimiros gave me a job, a good wage and taught me the ways of the world. He's been like an uncle to me and you like an aunt, as if you were my mother's own sister. Whenever terrible things happened to the Turks, you consoled me, and who knows how much you've protected me. God strike me down if I ever forget!"

As if they had previously agreed on what to say, the husband and wife said at exactly the same time, "You deserve it."

"Let's stop all this sad talk now, boss. Like you said, it's not as if I'm moving away. We'll just see each other less often, that's all. I know you want me to be successful and have my best interests at heart, that's why I need your advice."

Kiri Vladimiros bowed his head and then looked up straight into my eyes. "There'll be more and more people fleeing to Chania because of the Greek rebellions and all the murders and attacks on the Turks. All these new refugees will drive up the value of farmland, orchards, houses, shops – you name it. This job could earn you a lot of money, so that's one thing. If you're careful with it, it will be a great future for you. The second thing, and in my opinion, by far the most important is this: according to the rumours, some of the Turkish landowners here, or the top dogs in one way or another, are apparently sending money to Anatolia, to Kemal Pasha, who's fighting back the Greeks. They call them Unionists. When you start earning good money, you might end up helping them out as well – either of your own free will or because they ask you to. It's natural so I'm not going to say you should or you shouldn't. But if you do decide to help them, make sure it's absolutely secret. Don't give yourself away in idle chat."

I already knew this was going on and told him so: "I've heard two names mentioned – Tahmisçizade Macit Bey* and Alyotzade Mustafa Tevfik Bey. In fact, there were a couple more names mentioned as well but no one's sure about them. They say the money collected to support Mustafa Kemal Pasha is being sent to the Ottoman ambassador in Athens and Macit Bey is the one sorting it all out. The money goes from there to the Unionists. That's what I heard."

Vladimiros warned me again, "Whatever's going on, take heed of what I said. Be careful not to get involved and don't stick your head above the parapet. If you get caught, you'll be thrown off the island or killed. We want you to stay in one piece and make something of yourself, that's our greatest wish. Don't ever forget that!"

Just the day before, on the Friday, there had been a spate of murders as people were leaving mosques in Turkish villages. My fellow Muslims, my fellow Turks had been slaughtered again. Today there would be more families dressed in black and devastated with grief. But it would have been the height of cruelty at my farewell supper to mention it in front of these two caring elderly people, whose human kindness and wisdom were so far removed from all the religious and racial bigotry around us.

---

* A Cretan notable who later wrote *Girit Hataları: Memories of Crete*.

My mother believed that such people were worthy of heaven. She saw the world through the eyes of a simple village woman. But if it was down to me, after all the things suffered by our family and all the other Turks, I'd like to see statues made of these two wise souls – monuments to humanity, although I know it will never happen. After dinner, when the time came to part, we hugged and kissed each other, all three of us welling with tears.

15

In 1920, the news that our enemies were to carve up Anatolia between themselves travelled across to Crete in a flash. For the Greeks, the Treaty of Sevres* sparked ecstatic celebrations and festivities. For the Turks it was bad news, but we said nothing. We feared that the swagger and triumphalism of the island Greeks would get even worse. For all of us in the cities, it was as if we were sleepwalking through a nightmare. Even my business partner, Madam Maria, seemed unsure how to react although I heard that Kiri Vladimiros had spoken to her about it. Somehow, with her female adeptness, she hid her discomfort and succeeded in keeping our relationship on an even keel. The island Turks had been hounded from their homes, they had lost their land and seen their property burnt and desecrated. Now those of us that had survived faced a different threat: a campaign to assimilate us. Venizelos, the wiliest of the Cretan Greeks, announced, "It's time to stop

---

* Treaty which abolished the Ottoman Empire and divided up its former territories, including Anatolia. Eventually replaced by the Treaty of Lausanne after the Turkish War of Independence in 1923.

chasing the Turks away, now you should marry your daughters to their men." In other words, he thought he could Hellenise us until we melted away. Not everyone agreed with him; his opponents accused him of being a stooge to the Turks and took over the attack with their slogan, "First I am a Christian, then I am a Greek!" Either the bigoted Greeks had forgotten that Venizelos had led their recent victorious uprising, or they were in denial about it.

With the recent repeated forced migrations within the island, we saw history repeating itself.

"Ali Agha," they had shouted, cutting across our path as we fled our village in a convoy all those years ago, "what's this, an imperial procession?"

The tailor, Hüseyin Agha, who was working as a farmhand at Kukunara Farm on the outskirts of the city, had reached the end of his tether when he was threatened by Greeks whilst gathering olives with his family and other farm workers. He loaded up all their possessions on to the two-wheel carts we called *dalika* and set off for the city at dusk. The scornful words of the Greeks who stopped him on the road were almost identical to the words the armed bandits had mocked us with so long ago, still in currency despite the passage of time: "Hüseyin Agha, what a magnificent procession you'll be entering the city with!"

We did our best to get on with our lives by trying to bury the pain of countless insults like this. Earning money had become my main aim in life. A failure to do so would mean that as a grown man, I would have to wait in the queue for one plate of food at the door of the dervish lodge run by Mehmed Şemseddin Efendi.* How would I ever explain that to my mother, my sister's family, Kemalettin Bey in the POW camp, not to mention Kiri Vladimiros and his wife, or Hüsnüye, who I generally saw only on Saturdays since starting my new job?

While I addressed my business partner as Kiriya Maria, the Greeks affectionately called her Marigo. She was a dignified, well-read woman who never went out into the street without a hat on and always dressed with real panache. She cut quite an imposing figure with her huge breasts, dusky skin and raven hair. Each day she read both Chania newspapers, kept a keen eye on all the city's business and tried to keep up with events.

If anyone had asked me who was the prettiest between Kiriya Maria and Hüsnüye, I would undoubtedly have answered, Hüsnüye. With her soft, fair skin, flowing black curls and charming charisma, she was undisputedly a sensual woman and a great drinking companion as well. After three glasses of wine, she became more lustful, murmuring seductively as an overture to unconstrained passion. But whatever happened, she never failed to prepare us a fine table of meze and only sat down for dinner after fixing her make-up and recomposing her dress.

My business partnership with Kiriya Maria lasted three years. Throughout the first two and a half years, she kept her distance from me and our interactions were formal and

---

* A Sufi historian who travelled extensively in the former Ottoman lands, including Crete and the nearby islands. He wrote a travelogue called *Dildâr-ı Şemsî*.

respectful. I addressed her as Kiriya and she addressed me as Kiri. Every day except for Sunday, I knocked at her door around 9 a.m. and waited for her to open the door from upstairs so I could run through the day's business and get her views on any sales and purchases, all the while remaining downstairs while she called down from the landing. The lawyer Varuchakis was our first port of call when we had difficult issues to deal with. Some of our dealings necessitated payment in instalments and I would go to him to ensure we didn't lose any money.

We were making good money from brokering real estate deals on buildings and land, but our main income was from buying houses on the cheap with Kiriya Maria's money, hiring tradesmen to restore them and then selling them on at a good price. The city was filling up quickly due to all the internal migration. The new arrivals needed to find a place to live. Those who had been able to gather up their life savings of Ottoman gold before fleeing their villages wanted fields to farm; it was the only work they knew. We negotiated fields, orchards and olive groves for them, or sold them vacant land we had bought previously in anticipation of future profits. As well as the sales within the city, I sometimes had to walk to the surrounding fields and back two or three times a day to show them to potential buyers. A sturdy but stylish walking cane became my constant companion on these trips. While it was partly to protect myself against snakes and any other poisonous creatures along the way, it was also to guard against malicious human beings. In time, the walking cane became an inseparable part of my outfit and I thought it added a certain gravitas to my daily dealings. My mother was overjoyed, not just at seeing me earn good money, but also at seeing me go about my business dressed like a debonair city swell.

"You've done well!" she used to say. "You can read and write, you're a gentleman and you provide for all your family too. Your sister always prays for you because of the help you've given her."

"I haven't done anything special, just what needed to be done. You've had a lot to deal with so just enjoy it and don't be sad about anything."

"And if I could get you married off too, there wouldn't be anything better!"

I couldn't reply positively to this wish of my mother, because she wanted to break the bond between Hüsnüye and me. Attempting to drive me away from her, she would repeat the typical, scornful, Cretan slurs about people whose ancestors were North African.

"It's time you got away from that *halihut* woman," was one of her remarks. "Halihut" was a nonsense word, but I guessed it was a way of looking down on the North Africans and referred to the monotone sound they made when they lifted their hands to their lips in joy or grief. However, it wasn't relevant to Hüsnüye, not even in the slightest degree. Her ancestors were from Africa – and that was all there was to it. She herself came from the poor seafaring district of Chania called Kumkapı and that should have been enough for my mother to accept her. I couldn't understand her attitude when she had come from nothing herself and had herself suffered so much for so long. Nevertheless, I never said anything as I didn't want to upset her.

16

I didn't neglect the two people who, more than anyone else, had helped us settle and make a life for ourselves in the new destination forced on us by the unstoppable internal turmoil of Crete. Every three to four weeks, I dropped in to see Kiri Vladimiros and Kiriya Evthimiya. On the days I was planning to visit, much to the delight of Kiriya Evthimiya, I sent over a plump fish or, if there were none available, a bunch of seasonal flowers or a basket of fresh mixed herbs and salad leaves. Knowing that these small gifts were a signal that I would be around to visit that evening, Kiriya Evthimiya would roll up her sleeves and set to in preparation of a delicious evening spread. When my work allowed it, I would go to the print house as it was closing and walk to the house together with Kiri Vladimiros. He had now reached a considerable age and I sometimes linked arms to support him as we walked. The print-house employees looked on expressionless, unable to appreciate our relationship, and the sour-faced typesetter Vomvolakis, who had made his dislike of Turks clear to me from the start, shook his head disapprovingly whenever the opportunity arose.

Kiriya Evthimiya loved to meet us at the door. She doted on her husband. The two hours we sat around the table were as enjoyable and relaxing for me as they were for them. For we Turks, becoming an island minority after our forefathers had ruled the roost for so many years was an open wound. But rather than deepening that wound, it felt as if Kiri Vladimiros was inserting his keen blade to lance the poison. His education, wisdom and clear reasoning had a calming effect on me, giving me the strength to carry on the struggle and sending me home with a bolder heart. Kiriya Evthimiya was always delighted that I had accompanied her beloved husband home and excited that I would be spending the evening at their table. She couldn't tolerate any space on my plate, always filling it with another morsel, saying, "You haven't tasted this yet," or "You haven't had any of that." I knew full well that the appetising display adorning the table on those evenings had been prepared especially for me as she placed barely more than a mouthful on to the plate of her husband.

"Vladimir, don't be upset with me. I'm only giving you this much because I'm thinking of your health. I don't want to lose you. Stop looking at Hassanaki's plate – he's still young. He can eat what he likes now, but he'll have to cut down when he's older as well."

I was working hard to look after my family and, with an eye to the future, I was also occupied with buying and renovating houses whenever possible. But in the background, I was aware of some significant developments, such as the request by the Ottoman ambassador in Athens that Macit Bey arrange a consignment of money from Crete for Enver Pasha's brother, Nuri Pasha,* who was stuck with his legion between Egypt and Tripoli.† Realising what was happening, the British captured Macit Bey mid-ocean on his way back from Athens on a ferry he had boarded with the help of a French warship. First, he was sent to Malta and then, twenty-seven months later, he was transferred to Alexandria to stand trial. He was released after the trial and returned to Crete. It was the day he arrived back on the island, when I was planning to welcome him home, that I received some terrible news that pierced my heart like a bullet: "Kiriya Evthimiya's dead!"

I couldn't believe that the kind, jolly Kiriya Evthimiya was suddenly gone. My world collapsed. The area around their home teemed with the comings and goings of tearful neighbours. I found Kiri Vladimiros crumpled in a chair in the corner. We embraced. I felt the streams of our tears flow together into a great river as we gripped each other tightly. The women there prized us apart. We sat with her all night, staying until the priest came to make preparations for the religious rites in the morning. Kiriya Evthimiya's world had been changed by a sudden heart attack, but even in death she looked cheerful, as if she were saying, "Don't neglect your old boss. Drop by and check up on him now and again."

The church was bursting with people attending her ceremony, those who remembered Kiriya Evthimiya's warm, cheery face and others who knew Vladimiros through business, their bodies squeezed in all the way to the door. As the coffin was

---

* Ottoman Captain Nuri Efendi was sent to Libya with gold to organise operations against Italian and British forces.
† Egypt and Tripoli were part of the Ottoman Empire.

covered in earth, my heart bled at the sight of Vladimiros, the dignified, sharp-witted man who had taught me so much about life. He seemed to have shrunk in stature and his hair looked even greyer. The foreman of the print house held one arm and I the other, but we could barely keep him on his feet. That night I didn't leave his side. In the morning, I knocked on the neighbours' doors to ask if they could help me find a woman to take care of the housework and look after him. They found someone. In less than two hours, there was a knock at the door and a neighbour arrived with a lean, sprightly woman a little older than Aunt Evthimiya. I handed Kiri Vladimiros over to her care. After that, we would be together every weekend, but he had to become accustomed to the meze from the taverna rather than the hand-prepared delights of Aunt Evthimiya, and adapt to my mother's different style of cooking on the days when he came to our home.

On the Saturday evening following Evthimiya's death, I met Vladimiros at the print house. Partly to keep him from dwelling on things and partly to relieve his loneliness, I took him to Nuri's taverna. As we made our way there, linking arms from time to time, who should we bump into but Daggerlad, whom I hadn't seen for several years. I was in a quandary. Here was the man who had filled us with courage when fear rose all around us like mist from the mountain slopes, who without batting an eye had stuck his knife into a slew of people. This madcap adventurer was suddenly standing in front of me! I was curious as to where he had been all this time, and apart from anything else, I owed him a debt of gratitude – for protecting us when we needed it, for buoying us up by offering his protection when we arrived in Chania. That was all well and good, but how was I to introduce him to the dear, elderly companion whose arm was linked through mine? How could I talk to him? My thoughts whirled: here I was with one man who killed and another who utterly opposed it, believing instead in mercy, although it was true that Daggerlad did not engage in wanton violence – far from it, his actions were provoked by retaliation to the revolts and murders of Turks.

Daggerlad flung his arms around me and I hugged him tightly. Introducing him as the man who had been our guardian when we fled the village, I invited him along to the taverna. The black ribbon that Vladimiros was wearing on his sleeve made it clear that he was in mourning. Daggerlad cut a very different figure with his Cretan laced headscarf, two knives sticking out from his waistband and *shalvar* breeches tucked into knee-length boots. My drinking companions Badoyan Mustafa and Grand Mehmed were waiting for us at the table. They knew I was bringing Vladimiros, but of course they knew nothing about Daggerlad. Ahmet Agha arrived after us. It was the first time Badoyan and Grand had met my old boss, whom they held in such high regard, and they made a big fuss of him. They were all soon engrossed in conversation, while I filled Daggerlad in on all I had been doing since we last met. Of course, I explained in detail how Vladimiros had looked out for me, how favourable he was towards Turks, in fact making no distinction between Greekness and Turkishness, how he believed in humanity and was in favour of good relations between us all. I also told him about Kiriya Evthimiya, who had been a good person just like her husband, and had passed away just a week ago.

Visibly moved by what he had heard, Daggerlad turned to Kiri Vladimiros.

"Chief," he began, "it's the first time I've ever met a Greek like you, one who behaves like a human being. I believe that's how you are because it was told to me by the son of Ali Agha, God rest his soul. Until today, I've never kissed the hand of a Greek, but I will kiss the hand of anyone who's done and said what you have, anyone like you, who's as decent and untainted as the day they were born."

He immediately got to his feet, took the hand of Vladimiros and kissed it. Daggerlad's words and actions touched every one of us around the table, especially Vladimiros. One by one, Ahmet Agha, Badoyan and Grand kissed the old man's hand as well. Tears trickled down Vladimiros's cheeks on to his beard and he tried to dab them with his handkerchief, saying, "Bless you all. May God bless you with lots of children who respect you and kiss your hands. Anything I've said or the little things I've been able to do are nothing. To be more precise, they're things that come naturally to me. If the politicians, leaders and all the people of the islands thought like us and reflected it in their actions, we'd all be happy. And what happiness that would be! As beautiful as honey from the slopes of our biggest mountain, Psiloritis."

Nuri, the taverna owner, left his counter and came to our table. We rose our glasses into the air in unison and our hands reached for the meze together. Infected by the high spirits, Nuri grilled Spanish smoked herring for us. Placing it on the table, he said, "It's on the house."

17

The huge assortment of peoples and trades to be found in Splantzia Square made it the hub of Chania life. One of its finest features was our Hünkar mosque, which was later turned into a church when the Greeks took full control of the island. Regardless of whether it was Muslim or Christian, it was a jewel in the crown of all faiths. Another of its famous spots was Floru's coffeehouse, with its friendly service and spacious, stylish layout. This was the venue for the most elaborate night entertainment during Ramadan, hosting the grandest tombola prizes, the funniest clowns and the best shadow plays. In all other months, the coffeehouse was where all the hookah smokers hung out. There were times when I didn't go in because of the sheer numbers of smokers and the constant burble of hookah pipes under dense clouds of tobacco smoke. However, I adored the sweet smell of the tobacco after it had passed through the water. On the glass shelf around the coffee stove was a line of about forty hookah vases. Their hoses hung on two arms-width wooden nails at the side of the shelf.

Some mornings Kiriya Maria and I had our business meetings in the coffeehouse, always sitting at the marble-top table closest to the door. If she wasn't at the table at our meeting time of 9 a.m., I would knock on the door of her nearby house and we would summarise the day's business in just a few sentences. On the days when she was in the coffeehouse, we discussed our business in more detail. When she spoke to me from the top landing of the stairs, her head was uncovered, but whenever we met in the coffeehouse, she wore one of her numerous different hats. She had eight hats that she sent to Frangakis the milliner every five or six months to be laundered. When it came to her taste in hats, she surpassed all the other wealthy Greek women of Chania. I had a good idea about the way people spruced themselves up as my work regularly took me from one end of the city to another, and I observed them strutting down the street or rumbling past in their phaetons.

It was not just wealth that characterised Kiriya Maria, she was also an educated, clever woman. Even way back in those days, on the rare occasions that she joined me in the coffeehouse, she brought along the previous day's copies of the two Chania newspapers and read out the for-sale advertisements, municipal notices and decrees, explaining what we would try to buy from where and which properties we should try to sell. My boss and business partner, whom I now addressed like the Greeks as Kiriya Marigo, was in every aspect an impressive woman. She was also generous. A year after I started working for her, the two modest properties next to our home in Veneti Kastana came up for sale. Even with all my savings I couldn't afford one, but with her additional support, for which she wanted nothing in return, I was able to buy both in one go. With her help, we went from one house to three overnight. I had them renovated and rented them out a few months later. I even had a drinking fountain fitted to the outside of one property, which provided water for our whole neighbourhood.

After a time, due to the extraordinary increase in our work, it became clear that our brief meetings by the stairs or at the coffeehouse were not enough, and we rented an office in a street right by Splantzia Square. One table and five typical Cretan wicker chairs were all we needed. After that, people wanting to buy and sell came to the office to find us. When we needed to show land and buildings to potential buyers, Kiriya Marigo stayed in the office, while I set out with my walking cane to try and make a sale. We had a different strategy when it came to purchasing: I would whisper the real value of the land to Kiriya Marigo and the rest was up to her. She drove a hard bargain with feminine gentility, and her astuteness always ensured us a good deal. The properties we bought for a song later returned us high profits.

All the while, there was no sign of a let-up in the relentless violence and killings. Mustafa Kemal Pasha had completely emptied Anatolia of Greeks, chasing them back as far as Izmir. This news, together with the spectacle of Anatolian Greeks arriving as refugees in Crete, incited more murders of Turks in the city and surrounding fields and farms; those they didn't kill were beaten half to death. The violence that seemed for a while to have subsided and calmed, was now on the rise. At the same time, a declaration bearing the signature of Fağfurizade Hüseyin Nesimi* was circulated by the Muslim Committee: "Oh Muslim people," it began, "from now on, you are permitted to carry any type of weapon to use for the protection of our religion, our people and our honour!"

But that wasn't the end of it, despite Hüseyin Nesimi and the Qadi going along to the Greek municipal governor to inform him of the declaration. It made no difference, the violence continued unabated. We were living through a hidden but very real civil war.

In the middle of this turmoil, I was dealt another blow. My mother, whom I loved more than life itself, became paralysed. Nazire came to stay with us to help out but three days later, my mother died. This time it was the wizened Kiri Vladimiros who supported me. I remember him leaning towards me saying, "We lost Evthimiya and then Zeynep, now we're completely orphaned, Hassanaki, both of us. There'll be no more merry evenings round the table."

In all the time Kiriya Marigo and I had known each other, this was the first time she made physical contact with me. She linked her arm with mine in a natural, sincere gesture, clasped my hand in hers and said, loud enough for all to hear, "Try not to be sad. It's God's work. You loved and respected her when she was alive. You took good care of her. This is the way of the world. God rest her soul."

---

* A Cretan Ottoman bureaucrat who was later killed because he opposed the Armenian deportations and tried to protect some Armenians.

Amongst those who came to the funeral, I came across an old friend, Zambetula Ismail.* He had fled to Benghazi after seriously injuring a Greek; apparently the Greek had been pestering a foreign singer called Zambetta whom Ismail had taken up with. Ismail didn't stay long in Benghazi, but ended up spending a long time in prison. He was a dashing figure with aquamarine eyes and a handlebar moustache beneath his fez and always dressed in a plush waistcoat with a chain watch. In the days following my mother's funeral, some swashbuckling Greeks tried to set up a raid on the café he'd opened in Splantzia Square. They lived to regret it as Ismail had hidden one of the famous Gra pistols in a purpose-built cove next to his stove, ready to aim at would-be attackers within seconds. His fearless character in itself was enough to dissuade anyone else from meddling with him.

Although my lifestyle meant I was rarely home until late, my mother's death left a huge emptiness in my life. There was no longer anyone waiting for me to come home. As I approached home in the small hours of the morning, there was not even an oil lamp burning to light my way. My sister came to the house a few times a week to tidy up and do the laundry, but I still found myself at a loose end whenever I was home.

By this time, I was only visiting Hüsnüye once a week, if that, sometimes even as little as once every ten to fifteen days. She had taught me everything about physical love and lived it with me, but now I only slipped off secretly to see her on the days when memories of her lust took hold of me.

---

* Zambetula Ismail ran a coffeehouse in Chania and opened one in Ayvalık after the deportations.

It was almost out of habit, and of course, this angered her, sometimes driving her into a rage.

I tried to work out why I was gradually drifting away from Hüsnüye, but I couldn't quite find a reason. I was still attracted to her fair, marble skin and her sensuality, but she had none of Kiriya Marigo's solemnity, which everyone remarked on, not just me. I couldn't help but compare her to the well-read Kiriya Marigo with her milky-coffee complexion. Hüsnüye had none of these qualities. Could that have been why I was growing distant from her? I didn't know.

Hüsnüye had trim little breasts whereas Marigo's were huge. The tone of Marigo's voice, the way she was with people… maybe it was all of these things or maybe none at all. I was caught in a great dilemma. Could it be that I had fallen in love with this woman and her elaborate hats, who was often at my side for hours a day and who I had been working with for two and a half years now? When I asked myself this question, I was unable to answer. At times I scolded myself in shame as I admitted to comparing Hüsnüye's boisterous flamboyance with the silent stillness of Marigo's looks and her low, tranquil tones as she spoke. Hüsnüye was clearly more beautiful and enticing, what was wrong with me? Was it because I was spending such long periods of time with Kiriya Marigo that I was seeing less of Hüsnüye?

While I was immersed in my work and the quandaries of my head, the day also came to say goodbye to a friend: Mustafa Kemal Pasha's government had negotiated with the Red Cross to secure the release of my friend and Turkish teacher, Kemalettin of Bursa, and send him home. We walked as far as the ferry together and I stayed there at the port until it disappeared from view. He was so overjoyed at returning home to his family, and because the enemies had been thrown from Anatolia, that he could hardly keep still for one second.

"If there's peace, I'll come and find you, Hassan. You take good care of yourself."

"I'll miss you, Kemalettin Bey. I'll miss you a lot."

"I'll miss you a lot too, Hassan. I want you to know that I'll never forget you. You tried hard to make me forget I was exiled. You brought me food when you hardly had money to feed yourself."

"No, Kemalettin, the things you did for me were more valuable. I didn't know my own language and you tried to teach it to me; now I can honestly say that I speak Turkish. And even more, you gave me sound advice when I was trying to lay down roots in a homeland where I've become part of a minority. You showed me the way."

Kemalettin saved his most difficult and shocking words until the last minute: "I've heard some news that still hasn't got around the island. I said just now that if there's peace I'll come and find you, but the reality is this, Hassan: Venizelos, the man who's more responsible than anyone for the uprisings that tore this land from our hands, has been to Switzerland, to a place called Lausanne. He signed an agreement with the Turks, with Ismet Pasha, on behalf of the Greeks. In other words, after all these years of fighting, they've raised the white flag. But it looks like the victory means that you island Turks are going to be ripped from your roots again. There's going to be a population exchange and I'll tell you how it'll work – about one, one and a half million Greeks still living in Anatolia are going to be deported to Greece and in return, all the Turks here on the island and in Macedonia will be moved to Turkey... Don't pass out, brother! Europe made a mistake playing their greedy game to expand Greece and make it richer. It went wrong, and you and I have paid the price, and we'll keep on paying it. It's that simple."

Stunned, I said, "I was sad enough about losing you and now it's even worse. I can't believe it."

Kemalettin replied, "I'm guessing that package in your hand is for me – did you get your sister to make me something up for the journey? Come on, you'd better give it to me, the whistle's going. And don't worry, if what I said does turn out to be true, wherever you end up in Anatolia, I'll come and find you. Speak to Vladimiros Efendi as well and see what he says about it all."

The steamer filled up with people, the ropes were raised, and it began to move away, billowing clouds of black smoke. He was on his way home. The steamer became a dot and then it was lost. I looked on blankly.

18

Badoyan Mustafa, Grand Mehmed and Shahap Bey, a farmer who had joined our group much later on, thought we should leave the island. Their property was constantly being damaged by mobs, and as they only knew how to work the land, they had no chance of setting up any other business in the turmoil of the island. They were absolutely right when they said, "We can do the same job in the motherland without living in fear."

However, I thought differently, along with my sister and brother-in-law, Ahmet Agha and even the tavern owner Nuri and Aunt Cemile, whose husband Mullah Mavruk had now passed away. This was our homeland; whatever the cost we shouldn't have to leave. When I broached the subject with Hüsnüye, she was shocked and distressed, eventually breaking down into relentless sobs. What kind of life could she have in an unknown place? What did they mean by homeland? This was the place where she had first opened her eyes, where she grew and blossomed. This was her home, and she was making a good living from the rents – what else was homeland supposed to mean? What more did people want from her?

That was exactly how all those who favoured staying thought. But wanting to stay didn't mean they weren't worried. I tried to placate them with bits of information I had picked up from Kemalettin Bey and Kiri Vladimiros, or with the humble explanations I cobbled together in my own head. Obviously, it was true that pronouncements had been made, but that didn't necessarily mean they were going to happen. Why jump before you were pushed? Perhaps there was some misunderstanding about what had been said. Surely it couldn't be so easy to uproot that many people and, in exchange, take in all those who had been forced out by the other side?

I explained all this to them, trying to keep up their spirits, all the while with a huge lump in my throat and tears welling in my eyes. It was no use. The news was true, and eventually everyone on the island had heard about it. Very few Greeks expressed any regret about the expulsions. The rest could be divided into two groups: there were those who understood the suffering of being uprooted, but said nothing, choosing to keep their heads down, and, on the other hand, were those who already had their eyes set on the Turks' property.

I often asked myself which group Kiriya Marigo belonged to and each time I failed to come up with a convincing answer. She was a well-read woman of the world, but when it came to thinking of others or love for humanity, she was no Kiri Vladimiros. That was the conclusion I came to, based on her silence and general behaviour. We had worked together as business partners for several years, during which I had proved myself time and time again. Yet despite this, and despite the positive recommendations about my character that she had received from Kiri Vladimiros, she still kept me at a distance. The only signal of affection she had given was helping me to buy the two neighbouring houses. And I suppose she did that because I put my heart and soul into our business, not because she was fond of my beautiful eyes.

When the so-called Treaty of Lausanne* confirmed beyond doubt that, sooner or later, we would be taken from home and sent to our motherland, Kiriya Marigo began to seem increasingly preoccupied. Often, as we discussed business in the office, I would catch her eyes resting on me, completely lost in thought. On occasions, I felt the need to say something to her about it. "Kiriya Marigo, you're miles away!'

With a rare smile, she would reply, saying, "Sorry, I was lost in thought."

One afternoon, on a day I will never forget, with her face turned away from me towards the door, she said, "Aynakis, let's go back to my house and eat together. Ariadne will have cooked something or other."

It was the first time I had received such an invitation. I looked at her, speechless.

Ariadne was a gaunt woman, in her mid-twenties, who was still single. She rarely smiled. She moved slowly as she carried out all her solitary tasks, from cleaning the house to making food. In the room we had entered, at the centre of a

---

* Signed in 1923 between the Allies and the new government of Turkey, the Treaty of Lausanne replaced the Treaty of Sevres and redrew the boundaries of Turkey and the Middle East.

medium-sized table, was a plate of the courgette and cheese pie called *kolochtiha*. Judging by the smell in the room, it had just come out of the oven. Around it were three plates and three chairs, indicating that the invitation had been pre-planned. I couldn't help but ask, "I didn't know you knew how to make *kolochtiha*?"

Passing her hat to Ariadne, Kiriya Marigo replied: "We heard that the Turks made it and were curious, but weren't sure how it was made. Your mother gave us some when we went to your home to celebrate you buying the two houses. We loved it so much, we asked how to make it. She gave us a good lesson, I can even repeat it back to you. Let's see how well I learned…"

"Let's see!" I said, as she began to recite the recipe memorised from my late mother.

"Cut the courgettes, lengthways in thin slices as if you are going to fry them. If it's a juicy one, strain it in a colander. Make a dough of flour, olive oil, one egg and a pinch of bicarbonate of soda to make it rise, then roll out a thin sheet of pastry – enough to cover the bottom of the dish you're going to use. Grease the dish, lay the pastry in the bottom and sprinkle with olive oil and grated hard cheese. Fill it with layers of courgette dipped in flour and shaken lightly; the layers must be set at diagonals to each other and each one sprinkled with olive oil, cheese and black pepper. Finish off with olive oil, cheese and black pepper on the top, then cook in the oven at medium heat. Cook it for about forty-five minutes, or until the top is crusted or the colour of onion skin."

"You remembered everything, bravo!"

"We made it twice for ourselves to tease out any beginner's mistakes. Ariadne's become a *kolochtiha* expert. The third pie was the best one yet, so I wanted us to eat it together. Maybe it'll be your first *kolochtiha* since your mother died."

I remembered a final detail of the recipe: "You shouldn't scrimp on the cheese, but at the same time take care not to overdo it – don't be tempted to throw in all the leftover cheese on top to finish it off; if you make the top layer too thick, the bottom layer of courgette won't cook. That's the key to success… And making sure you use our good quality olive oil."

I was in fine spirits at being invited into the house for the first time in two and a half years and treated to a glorious courgette pie followed by delicious coffee. My contented and relaxed mood gave me the courage to indulge my curiosity about the house. A sizeable framed picture on the wall contained a photo of Kiriya Marigo and a man, as large as she was, with a huge moustache.

"That was our wedding photo," she explained. "We only had six months together – he had a heart problem that took him away. God bless him."

I left the house, making the excuse of two customers I was due to meet later in the afternoon. I couldn't bear to stay in the room with the photograph any longer, unable to stomach the thought of the flamboyant, curvaceous Marigo, in her delicate tulle-veil hat, being married to that man with the handlebar moustache. What a pity it was for such a magnificent woman!

As far as I understood she hadn't had the most stable of marriages. Perhaps that was why she was always so solemn? Neither was there any child from this short marriage of six months. I had noticed about thirty leather-bound books in the room. Was that how she had filled the years, by reading books alone?

Throughout our business partnership, which was now entering its third year, I had never seen any sign of her having a man. I mean, it was a subject I knew something of, albeit not a great deal. Yet, my knowledge and experience weren't getting me any nearer to a conclusion. She was four years older than me. She had needed to show her ID papers once when we were buying an olive grove in her name and, overcome by curiosity, I had taken a good look. Such an educated woman, in rude health, with a unique beauty and wealthy to boot, spending her nights, years without a man? Going through life without a man's ardour?

A storm began to rage inside me when I saw the photograph – no, it was more than a storm – it was a rebellion, and it intensified the fear of being exiled that gnawed away at me every day. Actually, it would be more accurate to say that it added insult to injury; Lausanne might have confirmed the expulsion of enemies from our motherland, but it sunk all of us island Turks into mourning at the thought of being torn from our roots. How could we be expected to leave our homes, our Crete?

Kiri Vladimiros had interpreted the routs in Anatolia as the price paid by the Greeks for trying to expand: "If you decide to cause trouble instead of getting along with people and living in peace, then you end up getting a beating. It's the poor wretched people who end up bearing the brunt of the mistakes made by their ancestors and those in power!"

Since the announcement of the exchanges, we had been living on borrowed time, and it crossed my mind to wonder whether we too were paying for the sins of our ancestors. One day, during my time at the print house, Vladimiros had showed me on a map how far the Greeks had expanded and how far they had later been pushed back. Then he showed me the growth and collapse of the Ottoman Empire... It was certainly time to wonder how far we would be pushed back as well. In the midst of all this pushing and shoving, it was us, the ordinary people, who were suffering, going hungry, losing our homes. "Nothing ever happens to the big wigs, Hassanaki," that's what Kiri Vladimiros used to say. "When they lose at their land-grabbing games, they say to their successors, 'Come on, now it's your turn to play. You can take the beating now!' On our side, it's the next king in line, on your side, another padishah in waiting! What a nice game, don't you think?"

19

It was Saturday. I had just returned to the city after showing some farmland to a potential buyer and was sitting in Floru's coffeehouse on the corner near our office. I had hardly begun to sip my coffee when I noticed the door to the office opening gently and saw Kiriya Marigo appear in front of it. I got up to welcome her over to the usual place at the table.

When she entered the coffeehouse, Marigo normally lifted the tulle veil on her hat or removed it completely. She didn't sit down. She was subdued and avoided my eyes. I could see that her smooth, dusky complexion was flushed red under the lace veil.

"No, I'm not staying," she began. "You sit down – you've been outside the city and you must be tired."

She came and stood right in front of me, her head bowed towards the floor. She never came to the office on Saturdays. Yet, here she was in front of me with her rosy face. Thrown off guard by her unusual behaviour, I waited silently, giving nothing away. I was puzzled by her flushed cheeks. Why was she blushing? Why was she standing there without saying a word? Why was her head stooped? Why was the strong woman I had become accustomed to suddenly behaving like a coy maiden? There had to be a good reason. The silence continued. Exasperated, I took off my fez and tossed it on to the table.

"Are you ill, Kiriya Marigo? Or is there something else wrong?"

She began to speak, neither lifting her head nor looking at me.

"Let's stop all this Kiri, Kiriya formality. It's just me and you in here. I need you. I can't explain now when a customer or the coffee boy might appear at any minute. Let's go to your house together in the evening when it gets dark. I'll tell you there. Don't ask me anything now. Wait for me here tonight. I don't want Ariadne to know where I'm going. We'll leave from here. Bring one of those dresses that your women wear, I'll slip it over my head and leave my hat here. I don't think anyone will recognise me in the dark. I'm going to go now."

After she left, I remained in a daze that lasted from the minute she departed until the minute she returned later. I bought a selection of foods from the market, before going home to lay a clean sheet over the bed and sort out the disorder of the kitchen. I didn't know why she was coming, but I knew it wouldn't be right for her to see the bachelor topsy-turvy of my home. Nazire came a couple of times a week to clean the house and collect my washing, but never on Saturdays. My business partner, the woman for whom I had the utmost admiration, had announced she was coming to my house; it was hard not to get lost in speculation.

No explanation I came up with was convincing. That she would come to my home and sleep with me – it was impossible, rubbish! That's how I spoke to myself. Obviously, there was something else she needed to talk to me about that she couldn't mention at the house, or the office. All the conjecture and dashing about, on top of a trip to the outskirts of the city and back, had tired me. Weary with anticipation, I lay down on the large floor-cushions at the entrance to the house, hoping for the impossible, my head full of half-waking half-sleeping dreams, and tried to relax. When I woke up, the light was starting to fade outside. I leapt up and grabbing one of my mother's *abaya* robes, rushed out into the street.

She arrived! We waited in the office until it was dark. We put her hat on the table and pulled the *abaya* over her together. As I was helping to adjust it around her face, in the way that our women wore it, she took my hands and clasped them in hers. This small movement so excited me that I trembled and felt weak at the knees. I could feel her breath on my face. "Don't tremble, Hassan," she whispered. "I need you. I need you."

We set off, walking just like the Turks, with me, the man, walking ahead and her a few paces behind. We avoided the open roads, walking via the side streets to my house in Veneti Kastana. My walking cane echoed in the darkness as we took care to avoid the glow of the corner lamps. She had held my hands in hers, she had said she needed me: the excitement pounded inside of me until eventually we arrived. When we entered the house, the small lamp I had left burning gave enough light for me to remove my fez, for her to remove her outer dress and for us to see each other.

"We're finally here," I said. "I don't think anyone saw us."

I looked straight into her eyes. They glittered against her flushed face like two black jewels.

"Welcome to my house, Kiriya Marigo. I know I'll never forget this evening. You gave me such a surprise and I'm still giddy with excitement. If I'm speaking out of turn then please forgive me. The first time you held my hand in yours was the day my mother died, and today when I was helping you cover your face, you took my hands again. Now I feel brave enough to take your hands in mine."

She jerked her hands away from mine, wrapped her arms around my neck and astonishingly fell upon me in a way that melted my whole body, without saying a word. Her lips were on my face, my mouth, my neck, kissing me everywhere.

To have expected more than this would have made me the most foolish of all God's creatures. I placed my left arm around her waist, pulled her towards me, and with my right hand began to caress the beautiful breasts I had at times caressed with my eyes. This heightened her arousal. By now we were both breathless. Then, she pulled away from me and began to undress as if she wanted to tear her clothing apart. We hadn't moved from the entrance to the house, and the gentle rush of air stirred by our movements was enough to make the wispy flame of the night-light quiver.

Here was the magnificent Kiriya Marigo, the woman I had admired from afar for all these years, at my house – with no hat, no veil, wearing nothing at all! She said nothing, her breasts rippling with the force of her breath, her nostrils flaring as if she wanted more air. I don't remember at which point she took off my jacket and shirt as we moved closer to the bedroom, or how she managed to pull off my grand boots, trousers and long johns. We fell together on to the bed, her on top of me and I felt her wetness as she immediately took me inside her. Her nipples had swelled to the size of hazelnuts and she seemed almost delirious, repeatedly gasping, "What's happening, what's happening to me…"

In the morning, at the first hint of sunrise, when the muezzin began the call to prayer, followed minutes later by the ringing of church bells, we left the house. I again walked in front and she a few steps behind, all the way to the door of her house. After leaving her there, I raced home and threw myself on to the bed, just removing my jacket and boots. We had been awake all night, opening up to each other about all the things we had not dared talk about during our years of acquaintance, interrupted twice more by passionate intimacy. The first time she had been firmly in control, but after that I relaxed, giving in to the instinctive experience I had forged under the guidance of the glamorous Hüsnüye; so much so that, after our last intimate union, the intensity of feeling caused her to briefly lose consciousness, driving me into a panic.

There was just one thing I couldn't be certain of, and that was whether we had been seen by anyone on our journey to and from the house. I hadn't noticed anyone, but it's not for nothing that they say love is blind. If anyone had seen us and began to talk, it would turn my life into a prison and rob me of this great love.

20

Life for the Turks in Chania, and consequently for the whole of Crete, was becoming harder and more terrifying every day. The refugees who had fled from the rout of Anatolia were attacking men they saw wearing a fez in the streets, even in the city centre, and the number of incidents was rising rapidly. When the attacks were reported to the police, they weren't taken seriously and no attempt was made to find the culprits. Outside the city, they would lie in wait for a suitable opportunity to murder Turks and plunder their fields and groves. It became an act of pure recklessness to leave the city alone, let alone without carrying a weapon; it required the utmost bravery. After the previous announcement of the Muslim Committee, sanctioning the carrying of weapons, I had bought a hunting rifle with cartridges and hung them up at home. Later, I bought a revolver and carried it around my waist, hidden under my jacket.

Everyone close to me was apprehensive. My sister, brother-in-law, Hüsnüye and Kiri Vladimiros were the most anxious, always worrying that something would happen to me. All the while I was seriously neglecting Hüsnüye, but I didn't know what to do. Marigo had mentioned to me that she knew all along what was going on between Hüsnüye and me. She had found out with the help of her lawyer, who made some enquiries about me when she was thinking of taking me on as a business partner.

As I write in my diary now, after so much water under the bridge, I recall the impact these two women had on my life each in their own way. From Hüsnüye, I learned how to please a woman intimately. She was illiterate and not greatly knowledgeable about the world, but with her I discovered the pleasure of drinking with a woman in private and the rapture of her handsome body on mine. It was Marigo who enabled me to have a more comfortable life, to become the owner of two houses and to enjoy the respectable status of a businessman in Chania. She showed me how intense a woman's lust can be after six years of celibacy. She told me how she had held her own against the Greeks who wanted to seduce her after the death of her husband, how she had resisted without exception and that this had gradually turned into a way of life for her. Her feelings began to change when she took to observing me from the window. As the feelings grew, she took me on as a business partner, yet in the two years we had worked side by side, she had not felt any signals from me, apart from the odd time she caught me stealing a glance at her. Naturally, the sudden news of deportations had thrown her into a panic. It was this panic, coupled with the years of sexual abstinence, that had brought us together. We withdrew from the outside world, meeting at her house for fear that we might be seen together in the streets. We began to spend the nights together in her bedroom. We no longer had anything to hide from Ariadne and were open with her. It seemed that she was also getting pleasure from our love life. Her sombre face lit up and a smile appeared on her lips when she spoke now. One night, I got up to visit the toilet after a fervent sexual encounter with Marigo, still naked as I presumed Ariadne would have long since gone to bed. But she was right there, standing to the side of our bedroom door. I froze in surprise, unable to go back into the bedroom. Unexpectedly caught listening at our door and confronted with my nakedness on top of that, Ariadne was rooted to the spot. A motionless, silent statue in the shadows, with her eyes fixed on my torso, laid bare for all to see. The faint glow from the night lamp on the hall table was enough to illuminate the lower part of my body in all its detail. When I came back from the toilet, Ariadne was gone.

I felt a change in me when squeezing the supple breasts and tight skin of Kiriya Marigo's dark beauty, so different from Hüsnüye's pale and soft body. Perhaps it was not so much a change, but she made me feel more playful. No doubt she had benefitted from having had a much older man in her late husband and never having given birth. She was fresh as a daisy, there was nothing worn-out about her. I wasn't sure if it was her true nature or something she had read in a book, but when we made love she used to swear like a sailor; one minute shouting out, bellowing the next, then whispering softly... She used to say: "Get going, you bastard, you're screwing a virgin here, for God's sake."

Maybe she was just drawing attention to her lithe body; that's how I saw it anyway.

The joy of our nights together waned every morning as the sun rose on a new day filled with thoughts of the migration and increasing acts of intimidation. It was now considered certain that we would be forced off the island. The Migration Commission was preparing the official documents. It was at this time that Marigo made her momentous proposition: "Hassan, this island is where you were born and bred. You love it here, you love it to distraction. Your family are buried here and you and I love each other. Become a Christian and stay here. Let's get married and have a happy life together. I'm taking quinine now to avoid pregnancy, but if we get married, I won't. I'll give you as many children as you want. I trust myself when it comes to that."

"It's impossible, Marigo," I said. "I love you and I love Crete – please forgive me, but I can't do it. I feel too much for my religion and my people. Come with me, let's go together and marry in Anatolia. You don't have to change your religion if you don't want to; I'd never interfere in that."

"I took a chance on everything. That's why I didn't want to tell you that some Greek bigots complained about me to Priest Agapios, saying I'm living with a Turk... with you. He came to the office one day when you were out. First, he said he was advising me but of course it ended in threats. I'll stay with you until the day they tear you away, not just from the island, but from my arms. I mean, until the day of the migration. After that, God knows."

Marigo was an honourable woman and never broached the subject again, just as she had never said anything, negative or otherwise, about her dead husband, and who knows what shortcomings his age may have left in their marriage. He was never mentioned, neither when we were alone together nor in her daily life – it was as if she had never lived as the wife of this old and, who knows how unsuitable, man.

The threat from Priest Agapios came to me too, via Ahmet Agha. Our group of friends still met together twice a week to share our sorrows, either at Nuri's, Renieri's, Bolari's or Pavli's place. We had plenty of tavernas, but for safety reasons, it was more often Nuri's place that we chose.

Ahmet Agha was more afraid than me.

"For the life of me, I just don't know what's best, Hassan. They'll do away with you... And throw your body in the water. Now the Commission is doing its work, the fanatics have got a free rein. They can take you wherever they want and get rid of you without leaving so much as a ripple on the water. You need to think about saving your skin. It's not a joke any more."

Was it a neighbour who had discovered our relationship? Was it Ariadne? Or Hüsnüye, whom I had been forced to abandon? There was no way of knowing where the rumours about me and Marigo had originated. But one thing was certain: it was a catastrophe.

Marigo's eyes became red and swollen from crying. She was unable to sleep. Finally, one evening when we were at her house, she announced her decision. I was not to set foot outside again until a passenger ferry came – and it must be Italian, not

Greek. She would make sure I left Crete alive – that was her wish. I was to travel by ship either to Alexandria in Egypt or to Brindisi in Italy. The route was up to me, but when and wherever I arrived, I was to use a Greek name to send a telegram letting her know. If I ran out of money, I was to let her know. She hadn't let on to me, but she had been frantically making plans because the threats were getting out of hand. I left the house just once after that, to finalise the official procedures to sell two of my houses to Marigo and transfer the other one to Nazire. Marigo brought out all her shiny Ottoman gold and divided it between three pouches so I could hide it under my clothes in different places on my body.

Mid-afternoon on a cheerless February day in 1923, at the Port of Souda in Chania, I boarded the San Marco ferry bound for Alexandria, feeling like an animal destined for the slaughterhouse. There was no one waiting for me with knives on the boat; they were all behind me now on terra firma. But the fanaticism that had driven me from my land, robbed me of everything I owned and separated me from the graves of my ancestors turned my stomach. I cursed all the events that had caused me to be there. In the fading light of evening, as I boarded a ferry for the first time, the sound of Greek words mixed in with the shouts in Italian filled me with dread. Here I was, leaving my home to go to the motherland, as if I would never come back again. There was no one there to wave me off; there was too much risk that I could be caught fleeing and killed in broad daylight on the shore. Although Marigo had planned everything down to the last detail, it had slipped her mind until the last minute that the fez I wore would give me away to my enemies. So she sent me off to the port, alone, in a phaeton she had ordered to wait for me three streets away from the house, saying, "I'll get a cap and bring it to the dock on a phaeton. I'll catch you up, there's time."

I boarded the boat. There was no one waving me off with a handkerchief, no one shedding tears and holding me tightly while saying goodbye. Marigo made it up the gang plank just in time, as the steamboat crew were making the final preparations for departure. We withdrew into a corner. She quickly took the fez from my head, then squashed and squeezed it into her bag. After placing the cap she had bought for me on to my head, she took a step backwards, examining me through wet, swollen eyes.

"It suits you," she said. "No one looking at you can possibly tell who you are or what's going on until you get to your destination. No one's going to bother you now. I'll go and see Kiri Vladimiros to explain why you had to leave suddenly. I'll ask him to think kindly of you, don't worry. It won't be often, but I'll visit him with some food from time to time. He's a sweet man. It'll relieve his loneliness and give us a chance to reminisce about you together."

I felt sick to the stomach. Frozen by the fear and trepidation of going into the unknown, I was unable to speak. She grabbed me by the collar, trying to bring me round, and gave her last words of advice: "Keep your money and travel papers somewhere safe. I spoke to some of the people who've come from Anatolia. They said the only place you'll be able to stay without any problems is a town called Ayvalık. Find out how to get there."

Out of view, in a recess of the deck, we held each other silently for the last time, both of us crying. I had lost my country, and I was on the way to my motherland in secret, passing through places I had never seen, and along who knows what dismal roads. Marigo was losing a successful business partner and a lover who could measure up to her at the pinnacle of her life and desire.

When I had come to the dock to send off my Turkish teacher, Kemalettin Bey, I had waited on the shore until the boat shrank into a dot on the horizon, then disappeared. This time it was me on the deck returning Marigo's waves, and as the steamboat moved away, it was Marigo becoming smaller, turning into a dot and then disappearing completely.

I can't begin to explain what a terrible time I had in Alexandria with the Egyptian peasants as I couldn't speak Arabic. They knew neither Turkish nor Greek. Marigo had said, "If you're having problems in any country, go to the port and you're bound to find a Greek somewhere around that you can ask to help with translation." I followed her advice and found a Greek cotton merchant, who helped me overcome my difficulties. It seemed it wasn't possible to travel from Alexandria to Izmir. First, I had to go to the Italian port of Brindisi and from there I would be able to get a boat to the Greek port of Piraeus, and from there on to Izmir.

Days later, I arrived in the cold, damp air of Brindisi. I found a room in a hotel used by sailors, and one night, I took a woman there. As I didn't know any Italian to tell her how much I appreciated her good company, I gave her a gold coin, but the hotel owner got wind of it and managed to wheedle one out of me for himself by constantly pestering me with his relentless Italian blather. My Greek came in useful at the port and I managed to find out how to get to Piraeus by way of a Greek sailor who showed me the way to the bureau of the right company.

In Piraeus, the coffeehouses and shipping bureaux, bursting with waiting passengers and unemployed sailors, smelt of sage tea and cognac. On the day of my arrival, I was able to get a ticket for a boat leaving for Izmir later that evening and before long I was on board settling into my cabin. It was a relief to be able to understand the languages around me once again, although it was overshadowed by the fear of being recognised by Chanians who might make trouble for me.

After managing my way around Piraeus, Izmir wasn't difficult for me. Despite the agonising resentment of being separated from my country and the woman I loved, I found myself feeling quite pleased, simply down to the Turkish I had learned from Kemalettin Bey. After being lost amongst the Arabic of Egypt and Italian of Brindisi, then being unnerved by hearing Greek again in Piraeus, the sound of Turkish all around was soothing.

The first thing I did after embarking at the Izmir dock in Kordon was to take off the cap on my head and replace it with a fez bought from a small place in the back streets of the nearby district of Punta. It was easy for me to find out where Ayvalık was and how to get to the place that was to be my new home. I had little difficulty buying a ticket and after one day and one night, I arrived in Ayvalık on a boat called *Hamidiye*, owned by Ali Bey, a banker from Edremit in Turkey.

When I walked from the boat on to the dock, I was stopped in my tracks by a military salute from a soldier of the Turkish army! Seeing my long boots, khaki trousers, chain watch, walking cane and fez, he must have thought I was an officer.*

THE END

---

* The dock that Hassan arrived at would have been teeming with people, some wearing all they owned, and speaking in different dialects of Greek or Turkish. The crowd would have consisted of people fleeing from many Greek islands or those being deported to them, all the result of the signing of The Lausanne Convention, which specified the conditions for the compulsory exchange of minority populations between the countries of Greece and Turkey and was signed on 30 January 1923. It was one of a number of legal instruments related to the Treaty of Lausanne.

GLOSSARY

abaya A full-length outer garment worn by some Muslim women

Agha A term of respect, literally means "master"

-akis Greek diminutive used as a token of affection or meaning "small". Surnames ending with -akis are normally associated with Crete

baglama A traditional instrument of Anatolian folk music

baklava A pastry filled with chopped nuts and soaked in honey

Bayram A generic Turkish term for a public holiday (not necessarily Eid and not necessarily Muslim. In the Cretan context, it may have taken on the meaning of a Muslim holiday and vice versa with yortu)

Bey Mr: Term of respect in Turkish, used after a forename

biberiye Turkish word for rosemary

fez A flat-topped conical red hat with a black tassel on top formerly worn by Turkish and other Muslim men

halihut From the Cretan expression "Halikoutides". An old derogatory term which is said to derive from the African command "Hal il kuti", meaning "put the box down", a phrase which was used among African porters. Africans were brought to Crete as slaves or came as economic migrants from the seventeenth century onwards. They worked mainly in the harbour and lived in shacks in the Chania district called Kumkapı which still exists today

Kiri/Kiriya Mr/Mrs: Term of respect in Greek, used before a forename

kipohorta Famous Cretan dish made from a type of leafy greens also called *kipohorta*

kitro A type of citron fruit

koliva Boiled wheat associated especially with a specific memorial event for the recently departed

Karamanlides Greek-Orthodox Christians in Central Anatolia (Turkey) who spoke Turkish as their primary language

Kumkapı In the mid-nineteenth century the area was a Bedouin village hosting 2–3,000 African immigrants that worked as porters, servants and boatmen

meze Appetiser dishes served as starters or accompaniments to alcohol

Noah's Pudding Also called "ashure". Pudding made of grains, fruit, dried fruit and nuts. There is a story that when Noah's Ark came to rest on Mount Ararat in Turkey, his family made a pudding to celebrate. They had very little food left and so made the pudding out of anything they could find

oka An Egyptian and former Turkish unit of weight, variable but now usually equal to approximately 1.3 kg (2¾ lb)

pasatempos snacks

Punta District of Izmir now called Alsancak

raki Alcoholic drink made of grapes and aniseed

shalvar Baggy trousers with a tapered ankle

Souda Souda Fortress was the last place on Crete to fly the Ottoman flag; the flag was taken down on 13 February 1913 by the crew of HMS *Yarmouth*, the last European warship to leave the port before the unification of Crete and Greece

Tarawih prayers Special prayers performed by some Muslims during the month of Ramadan

yashmak A type of veil worn by some Muslim women that covers all the face except the eyes

Yortu Christian feast